RainbeauHarley

Rainbeau Harley

Cerredwyn Horrigan

with illustrations by Robert Kelley

11-9-13

*To Stacey,
Thanks so
much for all the
support!*

Pigs Fly Press

Needham, Massachusetts

CR Horrigan

Published in the United States of America by Pigs Fly Press, 2013

Library of Congress Cataloging-in-Publication Data
Horrigan, Cerredwyn. Rainbeau Harley / Cerredwyn Horrigan. – First edition.
Summary: Fourteen-year-old Rainbeau Harley trades the freedom of ne-
glectful parents and her dream of becoming a tattoo artist for a wild road
trip from Eugene, Oregon to her grandmother's horse farm in Massachusetts.
Rainbeau learns to improvise, adapt, and overcome to gain what she desires most.
[1. Family—Fiction. 2. Tattoo—Fiction. 3. Allergies—Fiction. 4. Roadtrip—
Fiction 5. Horse—Fiction. 6. Oregon—Fiction. 7. Massachusetts—Fiction.]
1.Title.

ISBN 978-0-9888-013-0-1
ISBN 978-0-9888-013-2-5 (e-book)

Illustrations by Robert Kelley (rk9975381@gmail.com)
Cover Design by Michael Rohr (http://www.michaelrohrdesign.com)
Photography by J. Robert Williams (http://jrobertwilliams.com) &
Patrick Lewis Lowenstein (http://www.cgtextures.com)
Compositing by Chris Leiva (http://www.chris-leiva-portfolio.tumblr. com)
Cover Model: Alexis Myles

Contact the author at cerredwyn.com

Acknowledgments

To my beloved husband, Brian, who encourages me to learn and grow and change and who suffers through the pangs this causes. For your honesty, your patience, your love.

To my children, Wolf, Colin, and Brighid who help me grow. I love you all so very, very much.

To my Sage buddies: Maureen, Laura, Brian, Kristen, Jean, Olivia, Angela, Dottie, Leslie, Polly & Mike, Eileen, Allyssa, Mike, and of course, Panda. You are always there with love and laughter, offering help and hope.

To the incomparable Z, editing partner extraordinaire.

To Margie Lawson, über-talented teacher and editor and Tiffany Lawson Inman, the naked editor, — need I say more?

To Anne Mini whose harsh words helped create a competent writer.

To my critique group members: Susan, Joe, Hillary, Licia, Kathy, Katherine, Melissa, Betsy, and to my retreat and workshop partners who slogged through early versions offering advice and encouragement.

To my first readers: Marie, Diane, and Susan.

To Pam, Patty, Kari, and Tanya for your friendship. To Terrie, Pam, and the team at Visions for keeping me healthy. To my early writer friends and mentors: Burky, Solala, Christine, Jean, Peg, and Julie.

To my design team: Mike, Robert and Chris. And to Bob, Alexis, Julie, Jason and the folks at Creative Circle.

To Susan Corso: publisher, friend, sister in spirit.

To Stephen Schwartz, whose lyrics taught me to play with language.

To the many people who offered information or advice or encouragement.

To the reader: may reading Rainbeau Harley help you to better understand yourself and entertain you while doing so. Thank you for taking the journey with me.

My sincerest thanks to all of you.

To God. In gratitude. Always.

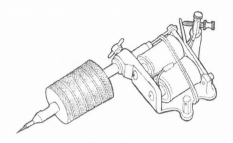

One

Why does my mom always have to be so irritating?

I'm stuck in our ancient forest-green Subaru with the cracked tan faux-leather poking the back of my knees. Eighth grade is over and I do not need another lecture.

My mother drones, "Feminism is the way of mindfulness."

"Mom, it's Buddhism."

"Buddhism, Feminism, Taoism, I embrace them all."

How about pessimism?

She continues to yammer. Does she care about the report card in my hand? Has she even asked to see it? No.

Is this the suck? Yes.

The suck – I sketch the words on my jeans in a tribal design, then sniff the grape-scented tip of my purple pen.

My mom is focused on my jeans, not the road.

"Watch out for that mailbox!"

She doesn't swerve or brake, but she misses it by maybe an inch. "Do you have to ruin that pair of pants, too?"

I finish the letter "k" and color it in.

We are so different. We don't dress alike. We don't think alike. We don't even look alike.

My mother, Star, carefree and braless, her skin pale peachy pink, thinks she's a fashion queen.

Me: soft frizzy hair forced into twenty-two braid submission, burnt umber brown skin, hazel-green eyes, and I know I'll never be in a fashion magazine.

Looking different, being different, doesn't matter. But why can't she care about what's important to me?

All I want is a real family. All I have is a Star and my Uncle Miles, All I catch is the end of my mom's sentence.

"... leave tomorrow," she says.

We always stay with her best buddy when Mom's manfriend of the moment, in this case Oyster-the-slime, moves out of our yurt.

She turns onto a one-way street, headed in the wrong direction. "We're going to your grandmother's in Massachusetts."

"Why?" The question explodes from my mouth accompanied by dramatic hand movements completely lost on my mom. "I've never even met my grandmother."

"We have to." Her voice is firm, not her usual pot-induced-anything-goes tone.

"I am not leaving Oregon. Summer is the only time it doesn't rain." Tires scrape along the curb as we stop. I grab my backpack, jump out, and slam the door. "I won't waste my summer vacation!"

My mom looks out the window at me. The lines around her blue eyes deepen, her smile faded to frown. "Rainbeau Louise Harley."

My voice falls to its standard level of annoyance. "What?" Rainbeau Harley I can live with, but Louise?

"It's not up to you," she says and drives away, barely missing an oncoming car.

The tension in my jaw travels to my stomach, guts roll as if I've eaten tofu that turned. Stomping up the Astroturf steps to my uncle's tattoo shop, I almost crush a blue egg nestled on the blades of artificial grass.

I wriggle my report card underneath the egg, tipping it into the hidden nest in the hanging fuchsia basket. No fingerprints, no cracks, no reason to think it won't grow up with its robin siblings.

Trumpet notes wail when I open the door. I feel a shimmer, the hair on my arms goosebumping erect. Flash covers the walls: bright-colored dragons, hard-edged guns, soft-feathered angel wings. A few of the drawings are mine and each time I see them my heart hip hops.

My cool combat veteran Uncle Miles, towers over me. "Hey, girl!" He pulls me into a quick sideways hug, his strong arm the same shade of brown as mine. "Early release from school on your last day?"

I step away and rest the back of my hand on my forehead, imitating the middle school drama queen. "The anguish and agony and cliques of eighth grade are over."

Eyebrow lifted, arm outstretched, toe tapping. "Where is it?" Uncle Miles never overlooks important things, like report cards.

I hand it over, the beads on my braids rattling, rattling like my insides. But no regrets for the hours I'd spent in the shop coloring flash before racing through my homework each night.

One long finger presses up on my chin until I look into his face, a smile darting from his eyes to his lips. "B- overall, an A in art. Not too shabby." Laughter rumbles beneath his words, "Except for the D in Phys Ed."

The breath I'd been holding comes out in a huff. "I'm no jock. And I am the only one in the family who is vertically challenged."

"But a D means you weren't trying."

Memory: standing in gym class, designing a tattoo from the wolverine symbol hanging on the wall, when a volleyball hits my head. "Okay, maybe next year I could try harder."

Uncle Miles heads for the back station, grabbing a bottle of cleanser. "I have the perfect end-of-year present, oh ye of small commitment."

On the tray table is a tattoo machine with his special needle configuration, purple nitrile non-latex gloves, and my favorite cobalt oxide color, zaffre. My heart is beating a full out drum solo, coursing through my veins until my fingers are tapping. Finally! Uncle Miles is going to give me a tattoo.

His grin shows off his front teeth, including the crooked one on the bottom. "Sit."

I bounce into the client seat, a real cushy version of a dentist's chair that can move in different directions.

"Hey!" He is pointing to the tattooist's chair.

My eyebrows rise and my muscles tense. "What?"

"Your first tattoo lesson."

"On you?" The weird thing is, my Uncle Miles's brown skin is a blank canvas. No tats. And that is really strange for someone in the biz.

Instead of answering, he gives me the tattoo machine. I've held it in my hand before. The square part rests in my palm, my finger on top of the piece that looks more like a carving tool than a pen.

He places an orange on the tray. "You can practice on this."

I force myself to swallow the stress stuck in my throat. "What am I supposed to draw?"

"Anything."

It's hard. The machine vibrates worse than the clippers I used to give my friend a buzz cut when we were ten. Press too hard and juice squirts at me, too light and not much shows on the rind. I haven't even tried the ink.

After about twenty minutes, I've covered the entire orange and mastered the pressure. The color is even, and the lines I've drawn aren't too shaky. Miles checks my work, a smile lurking in the corner of his mouth. "Ready for the real thing?"

Every molecule in my body screams, yes! Except my mind, which insists trading skin for orange peel is premature. "Really?" My voice trembles and I will it to be steady. "Now?"

Miles holds my left hand. "Try your middle finger. The nail is larger."

"You want me to tattoo my nail?"

"Why not?" Miles's raised eyebrow, the mark on the end of his question. "It'll grow out."

I press the buzzing tattoo machine against my fingernail. The blue ink spreads. Sucking in a breath through my mouth, I hold it until the line steadies.

Uncle Miles peers through his bug-eyed amplifying lenses. "How's it coming?"

I lift the tip. "It's hard to see what I'm doing."

He shifts the glasses onto my head. "Try these."

Better. Barely. My tongue creeps between my teeth. I grip the machine hard, the quivering frame wrapped around two coils makes my palm itch.

Pausing, I use a gauze pad to wipe off the excess cobalt. I finish the outline and begin to fill in the curve of the crescent moon. The vibrating needles skitter beyond the allotted space and I feel like a kindergartener who can't quite control her crayon.

My teeth sink into my tongue with the pressure and the reverb. At least the tattoo doesn't hurt.

Finished, my hand held out for judgment, I puff up with pride. "What do you think?" Dark blue against my tawny nail looks good.

"First try." Miles's voice is smooth from years of convincing capricious clients to have ink-dipped needles perforate their skin. He studies my tattoo. "Not bad."

He noticed the mistake: a cobalt drop hanging off the tip of the moon. I stroke the ball of my thumb across the nail. It isn't perfect, but it isn't permanent. I feel like doing a happy dance, but restrain myself in an attempt at professionalism.

Miles points at the feline wall clock, its eyes and tail twitching with the time. Time to get the shop ready for customers. He cleans his station: laying out the sketch, looking for his gloves, lining up colors. "Crowns and kanji and Celtic, oh my!"

I give my tray a spritz. The antiseptic smell of alcohol and

6

cleanser slinks up my nasal passages. My nose wrinkles to stifle a sneeze – there is no way I'll admit to Uncle Miles that his shop makes my allergies worse.

I walk over to his station. "Thanks, Miles."

He checks the needle configuration on his machine. "For what?"

I lean my cheek against his bald head. "Teaching me how to draw, letting me work in the shop." I hold up my hand. "This."

For the zillionth time, I wonder why Miles couldn't be my dad instead of his identical twin. His twin who is never around. His twin who prefers the rock stars he works with to me.

"You know your dad loves you, too."

I forgot Miles could read minds. Sometimes. "Right. Just not as much as being a roadie." Why did I get stuck with the loser twin for a dad?

"I've tried talking, lecturing, arguing with him." Miles places his machine on the tray. "Sorry. I'm the one who got the responsible half of the twin genes."

I kiss the stubble where a sideburn would be. Rubbing my fingernail across my lip, the new tattoo is rough against the sensitive skin. "You won't get into trouble, will you?"

A frown furrows his face. "Just don't tell anyone you did it here."

My eyes mirror his, hazel-green and worried. "I won't." Keeping it hidden will be easy, if I can convince Uncle Miles to let me be his flash-artist-receptionist-all-around-gopher this summer.

In fourteen years, I've learned one thing about adults: If you shoot for the stars you might just land on the moon. "You know

I'd rather be here, learning about tattooing than being stuck in a building with acne-ed, awkward adolescents."

"Illiteration not withstanding, we've discussed it before. Homeschooling is not an option." He grabs the spray bottle. "I can't teach you science and social studies."

"The Internet. I could learn archeology, theology, herpetology."

"Herpetology?"

"Snakes. Not the point. Whatever you don't know I can find out. I could even earn a high school diploma online."

"I do not want to homeschool you."

"But…"

"No buts."

Time for my moon landing. "Then can I spend the summer here?"

Miles plunks down like a trumpet note suddenly gone flat. "Tomorrow I'm closing the shop to go to TatCon." He scrubs the wooden desk until I seize the bottle of cleanser. It is not good for wood.

"No problem. I'll go with you." A grin presses on the inside of my cheeks. This is great, trade Grandma for TatCon.

He circles his finger through a puddle of cleanser. "I can't take you with me."

The words "Why not?" burst from my lips.

He grabs my hand and walks me to the mirror. "Look."

Okay, so I have a gluten-free cookie crumb on my chin leftover from lunch. He wipes it off, waiting.

I am not quite sure about the whole mirror/TatCon connection. "And your point?"

He turns me around to face him. "You're beautiful."

Weird. Very weird. A snort spews out of my small flat nose. Beautiful, even if it was true, which it definitely is not, what does that have to do with a tattoo convention? That is what my mind is asking. My too-wide mouth has another, less brilliant question. "Huh?"

Uncle Miles sighs so deep, it is as if a truth he buried long ago is being dredged up against his will. "Rainbeau, TatCon is filled with … unscrupulous people. You'd be fresh meat. I can't watch you, I can't keep you by me all the time." His hazel eyes darken, imploring me to understand. "I can't protect you."

Now I know why guys punch walls. I snatch my backpack, knuckles slamming into the edge of the desk. I feel punched in the gut, ready to curl around the pain. Instead, I force my taut-with-tension body out the door. "I. Can. Protect. Myself!"

Two

Outside, the Oregon drizzle settles on my braids. Why bother wiping it away?

Across the street, a family is huddled under a giant polka-dotted umbrella. The daughter holds up a strawberry ice cream cone and the dad licks off the drips. The son is so covered in chocolate, the mom could lick him instead of the cone. The parents laugh and share a chocolate-strawberry kiss.

A sense of longing, a dull ache in my chest, creeps toward my toes and fingers. I bring my thumb to my lips, but hook it through the backpack strap resting on my shoulder instead. This time, I will not bite my cuticles.

Block after block my feet hit the pavement in a rhythm to a refrain I've made up that is running through my brain:

Sometimes when you call me pretty
I just close my eyes and cry

You may think that it is silly
I just wonder why

Without thinking about where I am headed, I arrive at Amber's house, my second home after Miles's shop. Warmth, hugs, and happiness greet me.

So does the tooth and drool team.

My best friend hauls her dogs into the dining room and shuts the door tight. "You really should give them a chance. Miniature Pinschers thrive on attention."

"No thanks." A tremor of fear runs through me at the thought of the dog attack I endured when I was three. It may have gotten a mouthful of my coat instead of me, but I'm not going to let any beast get near enough for a taste of my flesh.

Amber gives me another hug to show she loves me more than the woofing wonders behind the closed door. "Why so glum?"

Only Amber would use a word like "glum". It is one of the things I love about her, that and the freckle/dimple combo. It's hard not to smile when she beams it at you. But the red highlights in her brown hair aren't the only reason I call her the Celtic Worrier.

In her room, I gather clothes from the desk, the chair, the floor, fold and put them away. A lime green shirt hangs from my fingertip. "This has to go. You've been wearing it since fifth grade."

She sits cross-legged on her bed with a giant plush panda, hugging it hard enough to pop a seam. "Piglets and little brown mice! You didn't answer me and you only clean my room when something is bothering you."

My throat tightens around the words I long to tell her. But I don't. "My best friend is going to Europe in two days. Without me. And she wonders what's bugging me?"

Amber puts down the panda and points to a box covered with plastic jewels and foam paint sitting on her nightstand. Two pairs of plain white sneakers squat on top. "I have a going away present for you." She picks up a sneaker and two tubes of fabric paint.

"I'm supposed to give you one."

"That's okay." Amber swirls aqua and amethyst on the toes of the sneaker. Hot glue gun in hand, she searches for matching plastic jewels.

Sitting with my back against the door, I sketch a flash version of her stuffed panda. Imagining the pen a tattoo machine, I press, but paper doesn't give like skin or orange peel. "You're so lucky to travel with your dads."

"Without my mom." Her voice is flat as a sequin.

"She loves you. She left you with two great dads."

"Loves me?" Amber's pale skin blotches. "A check at Christmas, a check on my birthday, so she can check me off her list?"

I spin the pencil round and round until the paper tears. Great. Now my best friend is angry. "Sorry."

Amber unplugs the glue gun. "It's okay." She holds out a sneaker. "Beau, non?"

"Bono?"

My question earns a flash of dimples. "*Beau* means beautiful. In French." She sets down the sneaker. "Let's go see the goofbuds."

Her dads are unloading groceries. Steve wraps his long arms around Amber and bends over to give her a squeeze.

Dominic hugs me, his bristly chin scratching my ear. "We need help making dinner."

Amber plucks two aprons from a drawer and throws one at me. "Prep chefs coming up." We wash our hands at the sink on the kitchen island.

Steve dices onions and rubs his eye patch. "How are things at the tattoo shop?"

From the top of the microwave, I grab a bamboo cutting board. "Okay. When are you coming down for a tat?"

Dominic points a large knife toward Steve's blind side. "Him?"

"Virgin skin it shall remain," Steve says, strutting across the kitchen.

If they were vegetables, Steve would be a zucchini and Dominic would be an acorn squash.

I slice the peppers in strips and dice them, contemplating the vegie-morph possibilities for Amber and me.

Steve leans over my pile. "And what is this?" He taps the middle finger on my left hand.

My cheeks and ears and neck get hot, but my brown skin hides the blush. "A rhomboid?"

Dominic throws the onions into the wok. "What?"

The whisper of a grin perches on Amber's mouth.

I hold up my hand. "A tattoo."

"We can see that," Steve says in a voice dry enough to suck the moisture out of a prune.

"I did it myself."

"Does your mom know?"

The beans need slicing. I get back to work and mumble,

"Not yet."

Dominic opens the refrigerator and comes to the rescue. "Fish or tofu?"

"Not," Steve clutches his chest in mock horror, "the dreaded white stuff!"

"Dad, you know Rainbeau's allergic to beef and chicken."

Dominic pokes his head up. "And turkey."

"And shellfish." Amber adds the last of the big four.

Steve sticks out his lip in a pout. "Po-o-ork?"

"Sorry, old man," Dominic says.

Steve points to his face and moves his hands down to his hips. "*Moi*? Old!"

Amber leans close. "Let's go set the table," she stage-whispers.

The tug of tension releases with each joke, with each tease. My shoulders settle and I relax into an evening with Amber and her dads.

After dinner, we play crazy eights. For once, Amber and I win. A sleep over at Amber's on the last day of school has been a tradition since second grade.

The next morning, the tantalizing smell of sizzling bacon brings us to the table for brunch. Her dads are already seated.

I pour a caramel-colored spiral of syrup on the gluten-free pancake they've made especially for me. "Did you know it takes forty gallons of sap to make one gallon of maple syrup?"

Dominic passes the casein-free butter to me. "Where did you learn that?"

I slather the ghee on my pancake. "Mom's manfriend number nine, the chef."

15

Steve hands me a plate of sausages. "What else did you learn?"

"Not a lot. He only lived with us a few weeks. Mom didn't like that he worked nights."

Amber grabs a sausage. "He was better than Oyster, number seventeen."

My stomach tightens around my allergen-free breakfast and I nibble on my cuticle before I can stop myself.

Dominic waves his hands in the air. "Oy vey, Oyster." He imitates his Jewish grandmother, "So who'd name himself Oyster?"

Steve spears a slice of bacon. "My dear," he says in a wealthy matron voice, "Oyster thinks he's a Rockefeller!"

"Not to mention," Dominic adds, "the horror of horrors: a mouse brown mullet!"

Steve smoothes his own wavy black hair. "Perhaps he's had the same haircut for forty years."

Amber and I are still grinning as we head to the kitchen for clean-up duty. When it passes inspection, we all get in the car and drive downtown to the Saturday Market.

We leave the dads on the farmer's block haggling over hydroponic heirloom tomatoes. Skirting around bushels of peas and baskets of strawberries, we cruise over to the plaza in front of the county courthouse. Swirling tie-dye, a fog of patchouli, and the rough rhythm of djembes, congas, and bongos fills the air.

Crossing Eighth Avenue, we jostle our way through the crowds by the food booths and head to the stage. A group of skanky teenagers are covering a Phish song. Amber shouts, "Do you want a smoothie?"

I nod and she melts into the sea of color surrounding us. A little blond kid, feet bare, hair unbrushed, hand outstretched, tugs on the hem of my t-shirt. A shake of my head and she toddles over to beg from someone else.

I clench and unclench my fists to the beat of the bass guitar. "What jerk would make their kid beg!"

The girl transfers something to a skeleton of a woman. Rapid eye movement, twitchy hands, sores on her face – definitely a tweaker. Why haven't Children's Services social workers saved this kid? But I know the answer. Steve said the courts are overwhelmed with meth cases. He should know, he works there.

I wish I could change things for that poor kid, but I can't think of any way to help.

Amber returns with our smoothies. "Let's go to the other block, where it won't be so noisy."

We cross Oak Street and sit on a low stonewall. A woman, gray hair flowing to her waist, strums a guitar. She smiles, eyes kind, front tooth missing.

Amber takes a big slurp. "The music's not bad."

"If you like Janis Joplin."

"Beats the baby Phishheads."

I pretend to lick my finger and draw an imaginary line in the air. We suck on our strawberry and spirulina shakes, watching the crowd.

"Star wants to visit her mom this summer." The words are out before my brain has sent the command to speak.

"Drive or fly?" Amber can be very practical.

"Drive, probably. I don't know if she's ever been on an airplane."

"Are you going?"

Do I have a choice? "Can you imagine being stuck in a car with her for three thousand miles? How many hours would that take?"

Her cup set aside, Amber closes her eyes and three seconds later says, "Sixty at Star's pace. She probably wouldn't drive more than six hours a day, so that would be ten days."

"No way." I drum my heels against the stones, counterpoint to the guitar. "The Star goes without the Rainbeau."

"Where will you stay?"

I swallow a lump that isn't spirulina. "Do you need a house sitter? I'll even take care of the MinPins."

Amber jumps off the wall. "Wow! You really are desperate." She carries both our cups to the recycling can, throwing the straws in the garbage. "Sorry. No way the goofbuds would allow it. What about Miles?"

I toss a quarter in the busker's guitar case. It's all I have on me. "He's closing the shop to go to TatCon. He won't take me with him."

Amber hooks her arm in mine. "Oyster is definitely not a possibility."

The thought of being alone with him makes me shiver.

We find her dads and squeeze together in a giant hug. My heart squishes, too.

My backpack has all my stuff and we are only a few blocks from the yurt. There's no reason to go home with them. But if I had a choice, I'd choose to be part of their family forever.

Three

Lights flash at the railroad tracks, the rhythm of the train lulling me into believing I can run beside it and leap on board. Seventy-seven, seventy-eight, seventy-nine. But all the doors are closed and the caboose rumbles past.

I stride past the "recycling center," twisted metal piled in forgotten heaps. Past the puppy mill yips and yaps. Each little nipper crying for a home.

My home is a round wooden building squatting behind the faded red Mercury Fury, its bumper surrendered to the ground. A Chevy Impala remains, rims resting on cinder blocks, next to a Ford Galaxie its headlight hanging ashamed. The vehicles are the only thing left of my mom's last manfriend. The one who taught me the difference between springs and struts and shocks.

I tramp through the vehicular graveyard to the door of the yurt. No working car, no bike. No one home.

As I cross the threshold, the garlic smell of pizza assaults me. I am so stupid. Why didn't I check behind the bushes?

Oyster, with his greasy brown seventies haircut, is in the kitchen, three steps away. Too-tight black jeans swing low under an overstretched stomach. "Hey!"

In the three months since he moved in, my intuition has shouted: don't be alone with him. I've listened.

Oyster thinks he's a pearl, but really he's just the slimy stuff that looks like snot.

I squeeze two words past my lips, "Mom here?"

His thumb and forefinger smooth the Vandyke on his cheeks and chin. "Food shopping. You know how long that takes."

Stepping backward, heart hammering a tattoo inside my chest, I reach for the knob.

He advances. One hairy arm grazes my breast, fingers pushing on the door.

Click.

My nostrils tremble with the scent of his body odor. I back away into the living room.

I could run for my room, but it doesn't have a door. I could dive through the open window, if I was a foot taller. I could scream, but none of the neighbors are nearby.

His tongue flickers on the edge of his mustache. A Komodo dragon contemplating its prey.

My muscles and tendons tighten, preparing for flight. Now, now, now! My body betrays me. I am frozen.

He stalks toward me, lips curled, leering over long, yellowed teeth.

My brain screams fly, fly away now! But all I can focus on is the crystal hanging from the center of the yurt's ceiling.

Slick fingers slither down the side of my face.

I long to escape to that small place buried deep within me. Where nothing hurts. Leave my body to suffer these groping hands, this hard-on.

His moist breath, garlic and anchovies, wets the tiny hairs on my cheek. His tongue strokes my neck, my jaw, my ear. Inside my ear.

Revulsion shivers through me. I slam my elbow into his ribs.

He grunts, expelling foul air and spit. "You little bitch!"

I slip away, bolting toward the door. A car door slams. I rush out of the yurt, gulping air. Palms pressed against my eyes. No tears, no tears.

My mother passes me, a grocery bag in each hand. "Hi, honey!"

I know she is talking to him, not me.

He lurches toward me. "Later." My mom looks at him, puzzled.

Inside, I am quivering worse than a tattoo machine. Outside, I am rooted to the earth.

Oyster points two fingers at his eyes and then at me. He smiles his rat-tooth-smile and hops on his bicycle that he'd hidden behind a bush.

My mom comes out to say goodbye, filling herself with Oyster's lies.

I rub my skin hard where he touched me. His essence lingers.

Into the yurt, I stumble to the bathroom, wet a towel and

slather it with lavender soap. Scrubbing my face and neck, purging the Oyster stench. My teeth brushed, I spit into the sink, again and again and again. I cannot tell my mom. There is one rule she always follows. Believe the boyfriend.

Back to my bedroom searching my stack-of-milk-crates dresser, I find the Louis Armstrong t-shirt my uncle gave me. It's so big I usually wear it as a nightgown. I stuff it and some other clothes in my pack. I need to see Miles before we leave.

I move toward the door. At the smell of leftover pizza, my stomach clenches, guts grabbed by a giant fist.

A cabinet is open. A brass urn crowds the cups and plates. Oyster keeps his mother's ashes in the cupboard.

The sour taste of stomach acid mingles with sweet revenge. I place the jar on the counter. It is lighter than I thought the gray soot and pieces of bone would weigh. Holding my breath, I lift the lid, stand on tiptoe, and peer inside. "Holy guacamole!"

I reach in, electricity pulsing down my arm.

Hundreds and hundreds and hundreds of dollars! I shove them deep into the pockets of my jeans and place the urn on the shelf. My heart feels small and hard in my chest and I don't care that when he finds out I've taken his money, Oyster will be angry enough to kill.

My mom comes in with another bag of groceries.

It feels like ants are marching up and down my skin. "I've gotta go."

I barely register that my mom is placing food in a cooler. "We're leaving soon."

Out the door, pack in hand, a shiver starts on my scalp and races down my spine. "I'll be at Miles's."

Adrenaline seeps out of me like oil in the car cemetery. I force my legs to carry me toward the shop, my head jerking over my shoulder every few strides. Scenes of the Oyster assault repeat in my mind over and over like the scratch in a rap.

The shop is crammed with the usual suspects. Eluding eye contact, I nudge my way between the biker dudes, the pierced Goth set, and the giggling grannies. Miles is finishing a sleeve, the last touches on the scales of a wrist-to-shoulder dragon. It's mid-June and I remember when he started the outline last September.

Joey, his assistant, is working the cash register. A Blue Oyster Cult t-shirt hangs on his six-foot-two frame, size fifteen hiking boots poke out from underneath the desk. He tugs at his ear gauge and nods toward the stool next to him. My head shifts from side to side, I'm not working today.

Imagining a force field surrounding me, I make it to the back room untouched. An afghan Miles and my dad's mom made before she died is lying on the old leather couch. I wrap myself in the soft knit squares of wisteria and jade and visit a shelf in my memory bank. Grammie Rose singing songs by Ella Fitzgerald.

An hour later, a tattoo machine clashes onto a stainless steel table. Miles's voice cuts through the noise of customers to the back room, "Remember, it will go through a peeling stage." He instructs his customer, "Do not pick at it."

A woman asks, "You're kidding, right?" Her words are warm with laughter, "You've done the whole sleeve and now you tell me."

I am trying to stuff the quilt into my pack, trying to hide it, trying to pretend everything is okay.

Miles enters the room and even with my back toward him, I can feel his concern. "Hey, kiddo, let's see your flash."

I dig out my sketchbook and hand it over.

He turns the pages: a rose perched on a barbed wire heart, a rainbow of dancing bears, kanji interwoven with a tribal design. He stops at the yin-yang symbol defined by two braided snakes. "Not bad. It needs work, though."

"You know the deal." Miles rips out the first three pictures. "Whenever a customer orders one, you get ten percent."

So far, I've made two hundred and forty dollars that I left at the yurt. Shoulders hunched, hands in my pockets, Oyster's cash presses against my thigh. I guess I don't need my money now.

"Are you okay?" Miles rests his hand on my back.

I can't help flinching.

"Whoa, girl, what's going on?"

"Nothing." I hate lying to him, but if I told him, he'd go all Mr. Protector on me and call the police. Police mean Children's Protective Services. For me. I refuse to lose my freedom to foster care.

I hike my pack onto my shoulder. "I'm going with Star." My voice is flat – a lid on the turmoil of feelings churning inside me. "To Massachusetts. To visit her mom."

He nods, his gaze the penetrating look reserved for combat vets and suspicious uncles. "I thought you'd be staying with Amber."

"She and her dads are going to Europe."

"And you're not hiding in her suitcase?"

If I could shrink small enough to fit, I would.

"Are you still mad at me about TatCon?"

"No." He was wrong. I can take care of myself.

But I'm lying. A niggling lizard of doubt reminds me things at the yurt could have been different.

He hugs me, kissing the top of my head.

I take a big breath of Miles: hand soap and sweat and funky cologne. A safe man smell. I hold that breath storing the feeling of safety inside me.

Why can't he skip TatCon so I can stay here? If I told him what happened, he would.

But I don't.

"Remember," he says, "improvise, adapt, and overcome."

My mom calls to me from the back door. She doesn't enter the shop. As if she's afraid that by crossing the threshold a tattoo will magically adhere to her skin. She's afraid of things that don't exist. And to the problems that do, she's oblivious.

I leave with my backpack bulging, my heart and hope shrinking. The car is loaded with blankets and boredom, pillows and passive resistance.

Clouds fill the sky, a myriad of grays. One thin shaft of sunlight escapes. I cling to its warmth, wishing my family was less transitory than the weather.

Four

I buckle my seatbelt, kick off my sneakers, and cross my legs. "You do know how to get there, don't you?" I ask my mom.

No response. She drives toward the freeway, fingers rigid, the Subaru spiraling down the approach ramp. She leans forward, squinting, voice tight. "What does that sign say?"

"The big one or the little one?"

"What little one?"

We've already driven past it.

Every twenty minutes or so, I ask my mom why we are going to grandmother's. No answer. Aren't parents supposed to get their teenagers to talk, not the other way around?

The radio is a welcome distraction. Until "Touch of Grey" by the Grateful Dead, blasts and my mom keeps time by tapping her foot on the gas pedal.

As the car lurches and slows in tempo, I hope we make a pit

stop soon. I didn't eat lunch, but maybe the gluten-free pancakes from breakfast will make a second appearance.

An hour later, we are twisting up the Cascade Mountains. The Willamette National Forest goes on forever, endless trees lining the road. At least she hasn't hit any. Yet.

In my sketchpad I draw planet "R" revolving around a star. A wave of nausea hits and I check the mirror to see if my skin has changed from sepia to sea green.

This trip is the itch of a peeling tattoo. Nothing I can do about it. I wriggle around until I am facing backwards. My mom doesn't even notice that I am no longer following safety belt regulations.

Nestled on a pillow is a plaster mask of her face, painted iridescent pink with a sequin on its chin. A gallon glass jar holds what looks like a giant pancake floating in weak coffee. My mother's kombucha — a symbiotic culture of bacteria and yeast. She claims the liquid from the scoby has been keeping her healthy for years. I'd rather catch a cold than drink that stuff.

A photo is wedged between the jar and a Buddha that resembles a toad. I grasp the frame with the tips of my two fingers and my shoulder pops. My mom didn't pack it in her bag, but I have that don't-touch-even-if-there's-no-reason-not-to feeling. I pick it up anyway.

My back turned toward her, I study my reflection in the picture's glass. Brown skin, braided hair, and hazel green eyes hover above the photo of my mom: fair, blue-eyed, and blond. A man with dark skin is hugging her.

He doesn't look like Miles, so it's not my dad. My mom doesn't keep his picture on display — it probably wouldn't be popular with her manfriends. My dad hasn't been around much and my memory is fuzzy. All I have left is a twinge of guilt. I still wonder if I'm the reason he left.

But if the guy in the photo isn't my dad, then who is he? Why haven't I seen him before? I scrutinize every detail of his face. He's way older than my mom.

When she turns her head, I shove the photo into the pocket of my backpack between my epipens and my emergency chocolate bar. The old yarn of Grammie's quilt is petal soft against my palm.

Star fiddles with the radio, a slow spin of the dial revealing only static. She turns it off and a thrum of tension fills the vacuum left by the noise.

Up, up, up. With each switchback, her knuckles turn a shade paler. I don't think she's blinked since we began. We drive over the Willamette Pass and I squirm and swivel. "Maybe we could stop."

"First, let's get out of the mountains."

The only sound is the whoosh of rubber meeting pavement. I breathe in the sharp evergreen scent, beyond ready for a break. "I saw a sign for the Salt Creek Waterfall."

My mom, mouth slightly open, looks too frazzled to argue. She's been driving for an hour and a half. How will we ever make it across the country?

We pull off Route 58 and park under the trees. I open the door and step onto pine needles. They scrunch under my bare feet when I walk to the driver's side.

My mother's head rests on the steering wheel.

"Breathe, Mom."

Stiff, she slides out of the Subaru. She lifts her foot and settles it onto her thigh, hands reaching toward the sky. Ugh. Tree pose. She is such a yoga geek.

I dig through the cooler, stashing tofu paté and rice crackers in my backpack. I slide the photo back into the spot by the Buddha/toad when my mom isn't looking.

We walk down the trail after paying to get closer to the Falls. Water thunders, releasing rainbows.

I am still and the world shifts.

The boom of my heart synchronizes with the force of the water. I understand with vibrant clarity that I am one with the waterfall, one with all that surrounds me, one tiny part of the whole universe. As if the boundaries of who I believe myself to be have no more substance than spray and mist. The feeling holds me, excites me, frightens me — fathomable and unfathomable.

Sinking cross-legged to the ground, I rummage through my backpack for my colored pencils and a pad. Deep browns and burnt siennas for the mountains, dark olive and hunter and pine, roughing in the trees. The Falls are white with flashes of azure and violet. I rub my tattoo against my lip, struggling to focus, to capture the power and the oneness.

I don't succeed.

My mom smoothes the frizz that has escaped my braids. "Your dad is creative, too."

Questions flit through my mind like hummingbirds. I seize one. "What was he like when you met?"

She whispers, "I fell in love with his eyes and he always made me laugh."

Seconds tick by.

"Mom?"

The wind blows straggling hairs around her face. She grasps the slick wooden rail and stares somewhere into the past. Silent.

The moment is gone.

"Why are we going to grandmother's?" I ask for the bazillionth time.

She hesitates, holding secrets.

"Mom, why are you dragging me all the way to Massachusetts?"

With the look she gives me, if my mother was a sorceress she would turn me into a toad, or maybe a Buddha.

Waiting. I consider the pencils I'd need to blend the exact colors of the stones at the bottom of the falls. Waiting. Nibbling a cuticle instead of a cracker. Waiting.

"My mother, your grandmother, is sick." The words squeak as if forced out against her will. "She asked me...us...to come see her."

"Sick? How sick?" Silence, but I cannot wait. "Mom!"

"She...she's dying."

"Dying?" The neurons in my brain grasp at the thought, but it wriggles away. "I don't even know her!"

She braids a strand of three long pine needles. "This is your chance."

A cross-country road trip to meet a grandmother who's dying. This is such a Star stunt. "It's going to take forever to drive."

She moves down the path, droplets of water resting on her hair. "We have time. The doctors gave her six months."

It better not take us that long to get to Massachusetts. I follow her and an argument starts somewhere in my chest and crawls up my throat. I shut my mouth, tight and the angry words slide back down. There is nothing to worry about. We will return in four weeks for the Fair: the hippy-dippy, clothes optional, dust-and-drug-fest. My mother wouldn't miss it for all the pot in Humboldt County. Well, for that, she might.

I tuck the uneaten paté into the cooler and climb into the car. Fingers of fear tighten, squeezing my throat. "What will I eat?"

She slides into the driver's seat, fiddling with the chopstick that keeps most of her hair in a bun. "There are grocery stores."

"The wrong food can kill me!"

"Don't worry about your food allergies."

"Look around! We're in the middle of the effing wilderness and we have three thousand miles to go!"

She starts the car. "It won't be this desolate everywhere."

Do they even eat tofu on the East Coast?

The road turns, twists, twines down the mountains, the heights flattening into foothills. The Subaru dawdles across Oregon's high desert, sand and sage stretch for miles.

After a mini-eternity, my mom barely pulls over to the side of the road before stopping the car. She gets out and rummages through her bag, flinging tie-dyed skirts, tie-dyed tights, tie-dyed shirts and the occasional piece of paisley. "Safety break!" Her code for getting high, but my mother is more into wrinkles than irony.

"Mom, we can stop in town." A large sign announces a Mosquito Festival nearby. Too bad it's not July. "Food, bathrooms – the necessities."

"I have my own necessities."

Slamming the car door when I get out doesn't even get her attention. "We can't stay in the middle of the road!"

She continues her search, focused as any beagle at an airport.

"We're nowhere!"

With the ecstatic look of an aging hippy at a Woodstock reunion, she pulls out a baggie holding matches, rolling papers, and green buds.

My voice is stuck between a plead and a whine, "This isn't Eugene. What if the cops see you?"

She lowers the trunk lid, barely missing my head. "Really?" she asks with obnoxious adult attitude. "We're nowhere. Remember?"

This is so stupid. "Mom, please don't."

She places a large pinch of marijuana on a paper – rolls, licks and twists. "I'll do whatever I want!"

My mom always does.

She lights the joint and takes a long hit. Holding her breath, she forces the smoke to stay in her lungs.

I walk into the desert, passing sage, mesquite, and the occasional cactus.

Why does my mom have to get high?

In a flash, I am four-years-old, needing to go pee, bad. My mom smiles as her friend passes her something. She takes a big breath and smoke swirls from her mouth and nose. A stinky feet smell fills the air. I am squirming, hopping from foot to foot, pulling on her shirt until my underpants are wet. Pee runs down my legs. The adult laughs. My mom laughs.

I am not laughing now. I am hunched down in the powdery dirt by a gray-green sage bush, arms wrapped around my knees. Tears splash on the sand, on my jeans, on my wrists. I cry until my sobs are dry and I gasp for air.

I have never asked my mom not to smoke, always knowing she'd choose the drugs, not me. I am empty – a husk ready to blow away with the tumbleweeds.

The shadows lengthen and the sun hurries behind the hills. I wait, hoping my mom will come and comfort me, knowing she won't.

A tan lizard with a blue throat patch scoots across a rock, racing for the safety of the sage brush. If I was a lizard, life would be simple. Except I'd have to eat bugs.

I slap the sand off my jeans and return to the car, exhausted by my pity party. Time to assess the damage.

Star sits in the middle of the road, her head pressed against the bumper, the empty cooler beside her. Marijuana smoke, smelling like skunk, lingers in the air.

I shake her shoulder, harder than necessary. "We have to go. It's getting late."

Eyes closed, a goofy grin plastered on her face, she dangles the keys. And drops them on the ground.

She is way too wasted to have smoked just pot. I shake her again, harder. "Mom, did you take some pills?" No answer. Just drool dribbling down her chin. I consider slapping her, but I doubt it would help.

After prying her fingers from the baggie, I open the ziplock, poke a sticky bud, and take a whiff. No strange smell, no powder, nothing obvious mixed in.

Bag turned upside down, the wind whisks the marijuana away. She won't be needing that anymore.

Her head rolls and she slumps to the asphalt with a thud.

My nerve endings tingle on high alert. Even my mom doesn't usually get this high.

The landscape is eerie in the light of the rising moon. Tiny rustlings sound all around me. What animals are awake at night in the desert? Owls? Coyotes? Bear?

What was it Miles said? Improvise, adapt, and overcome.

The thought of leaving my mother on the road briefly flicks through my brain, but I can't abandon her. We'll be safer in the car.

So I yank and heave and shove her into the back seat, pushing all the stuff she'd placed there onto the floor. The pink mask of her face falls, crushed beneath my foot.

I pick up the cooler and place it in the back. Tiny lights in the east reflect off the baggie on the ground, catching my attention. Our forest-green Subaru is not very visible in the dark.

I sit behind the wheel, my whole body is taut with tension. We cannot stay here.

The sun has sucked all the heat out of the world when it set. I try to put the car in gear, but it doesn't work. No matter how hard I force it, the shift stays stuck in park. The lights in the distance are brighter.

I am fourteen.

I shouldn't have to know how to drive.

I do not know how to drive.

My mouth is dry as the landscape surrounding me. I press my hands to the sides of my head. Think, think, think! My mind is empty.

The lights have doubled in size. They are growing. Growing to the size of sunflowers. Mesmerizing intensity, hiding danger.

The quiet voice inside me says, headlights. Pushing buttons, twisting knobs, flipping switches until I find the right one.

Moments later, the truck rushes past and our car shimmies on the pavement. The overlong blast of the horn electrifies me. But my mom is dead to the world, dead as her favorite band.

I pummel the steering wheel until the strikes become rhythmic and I recognize the song. I make up my own lyrics:

If only I knew how to drive
If only we weren't going to my grandmother's
If only...
If only my mom really loved me.

Five

The noise and jolt of a scraping and grinding bumps me awake. There is something poking my thigh. I begin fighting before my eyes are open.

It is only the gearshift as my mother drives over a speed bump.

My sleeping bag is cocooned around my legs. A birthday present from Miles when I was four and I've slept in it every night since. Who cares if it only comes up to my hips and is covered with a picture of a redheaded mermaid?

My mom points to my fingernail. "You could have told me."

It is morning. Thirteen hours since my mother's head hit the pavement and she's acting as if her "safety break" had never occurred.

"Told you before or after you got high?" I ask.

She pulls into a parking spot at a health food store. "I'm not a drug addict. You can talk to me."

What part of "drug addict" does she not understand? The part where you do drugs or the part where you prefer them to people you're supposed to love?

I slip my legs out of my mermaid bag, memories of last night returning. A frozen-in-time feeling clutches me as images reel through my brain of the high desert stretching for miles, my mom passed out on the road, and truck headlights blossoming in the dark.

I will never shake that feeling of fear behind the wheel. Drive a car? Not when I am fifteen and can get a permit, not when I am sixteen and can get a license, not when I am an adult. I will take the bus, train, walk, whatever. Four wheels on the ground and one in my hands – no way. I send the memories into the deep, dark, mawing pit of things I never-ever-the-rest-of-my-life-want-to-think-about-again.

Star leaps out of the car and opens her arms wide to embrace the sun. Next, she tips the glass jar with the scoby and pours some of the liquid into her piggy pink peace mug.

I drag myself out of the Subaru and she sticks the cup in my face.

"Yuck!" There is no way I am going to drink that bacteria yeasty thing, even if my mother does think it's a path to enlightenment.

Star takes a long slurp. "Where's my mask? The one with the sequin?"

"I don't know." This is not a lie. I have no idea where we were when I crushed it with my foot. There was sage there and there is sage here.

Breathing in the musty smell of the high desert, I wonder: Is nature God or did God create nature? I'll have to think about that when I am fully awake.

My mother chatters away as she spreads her yoga mat on the asphalt, taking up the spot next to our car. I ignore her, not that she notices.

A recreational vehicle, state stickers plastered along the side, lumbers into the parking lot. Massachusetts is missing from its map. Wish it was missing from mine.

How many days will it take to drive across the country? It hasn't been twenty-four hours yet and I'm already sick of traveling with my mom. "I thought you didn't like grandmother."

Hands on the ground, feet in the air in a downward-facing tree pose, she tips as if a lumberjack swiped the first cut with an ax. "She's not my favorite person, but I still want to see her if she…before she…"

"Dies. Wouldn't it be faster to fly?"

She flops down into full lotus. "I…do…not…fly."

I decide to press the issue, wanting an answer. No. What I really want is reassurance that last night won't happen again. "Why not? Maybe she doesn't have six months. We might not make it in time."

"Oh, we will." My mom presses her palms together and closes her eyes, shutting me out. The discussion is as over as the latest hot yoga fad.

Magical thinking. If Star believes something to be true, then to her it is. She refuses to see any evidence that contradicts her belief. She'll see it, when she believes it.

I prefer to be practical. Popping open the Subaru's hood, I make a mental checklist of all the things that could go wrong:

39

flat tire, radiator leak, brake failure. I am certain my mother started the trip without getting the car inspected.

I check the oil, glad one of us knows how, thanks to her autogeek manfriend. I wipe the grease off my hands and tuck the rag back in the corner of the engine, closing the hood.

A gray-haired couple in sandals and Hawaiian shirts step out of the RV and stare at my mother. They head for the Oasis Health Food Store with their yapping Chihuahua dressed in a clown suit.

"Mom, the freak show's over. The store's open." She still hasn't mentioned the fact that we're in Lakeview, Oregon, instead of on the highway in Nowhereville. Does she even remember what happened? Probably not.

She unpretzels herself from the pose, hard fingers tightly twisting her mat. Isn't yoga supposed to be a tension reliever?

I follow yippy dog and the clown masters into the Oasis. Cool air, smelling of stargazer lilies stacked by the door, surrounds me when I enter.

Ah, comfort food: buffalo jerky, hemp milk, and sunflower seed butter, soy cheese, fresh fruit, and veggies. I fill the cart, deciding that puffed millet and pomegranate juice can go, if my mom doesn't have enough cash. Oyster's wad is still in my pocket, but it's not for groceries.

At the checkout, my mom fishes a bill out of her waistband. It hangs from her fingers limp and sweaty. The clerk, eyes wide as a vegan in a butcher shop, hesitates before taking it.

"Mom, how long will it take us to get to Massachusetts?"

"A week, maybe," she answers. "Depending on your driving." Her smile doesn't tell me if she's kidding or not.

"No!" I hadn't meant to shout.

I grab the money and hand it to the checkout guy. Why is my mother so effing clueless?

I load the groceries in the car, fill the cooler – fruit on top. There definitely isn't enough food to last from West Coast to East.

We gas up at a nearby station and we're on our way, my mom singing, "Truckin' down to New…" Off-key, as usual.

"We're not headed to the South, are we?"

She risks a quick grin in my direction. "Why not?"

My voice hits a note higher than any in the song. "Louisiana!"

"Winnemucca."

"Win in Mecca?" Weird, even for my mom.

"Visiting an old friend."

We cross the state line into Nevada. I ask a zillion questions about my mom's life before she moved to Oregon. Her answer: Curiosity killed the cat. Good thing I'm not a feline or a long time ago, I'd have been dead.

A few hours later, my butt is smooshed into the car's upholstery and squirming doesn't help. "Mom, can't you drive faster than forty-five?"

Her foot bears down slightly and we are speeding along at fifty. We pass a sign for Winnemucca – 68 miles. If Amber was here she'd already be telling me exactly how many minutes it would take. If I was with her, I'd be on my way to Paris.

The only interesting thing we see between the scrub brush and the sage is a sign for the Virgin Mines. My mom refuses to stop, even after I explain that we could mine opals. Opals with colors shifting and transforming, my favorite gems.

Instead, we plod along. Winnemucca here we come!

We get off the highway and, for once, my mom seems to know the directions. "Look for Dane Street, number 312."

"Now can you tell me who we're visiting?" As if I haven't asked three hundred and eleven times before.

She pulls her shoulders up to her ears and lets out a giant sigh. "Bob is a carpenter. I met him when I was on the road."

My eyebrows rise so high they pull the skin on my cheekbones tight. "As in roadie? With a rock band?"

"I travelled with your dad and the band before you were born."

Not even an "hmm" passes my lips. My brain seems to have stopped working, except for one question repeating in an infinite loop: Why is it that no one has told me this story?

Another question pops into my mind, and another, and another filling my throat and mouth, until I spit one out. "Why are we visiting Bob?"

"Old times and . . ."

My head falls back against the seat with a thud. Pot. She has realized the baggie is gone. How could I think she didn't notice?

"There it is!" The car swerves to the right, just missing the Dane Street sign. Number 312 is two houses down, single-story, brown with tan shingles.

We pull into the driveway. A bear of a man stands in the door, his eyes slits against the bright sun. He takes two steps, stops and the corner of his mouth lifts the huge beard covering his jaw and neck. "Stargirl."

My mother leaps out of the car. "You got my message!"

I can see she wants to run to him, but his arms are crossed. Definitely awkward.

Covering his left forearm is a tattoo of a roaring bear, anatomically correct, male.

My mom points at me. "This is my daughter, Rainbeau."

I wave weakly from the seat, not sure I want the ursine ire to rise. Why doesn't my mom realize we are not wanted here? Instead she stands, a Starflower planted in the garden.

The big man squats down and picks a Black-Eyed Susan. The yellow petals scatter on the dried-out grass. "Star, you always did have the damnedest timing."

Is that good or bad?

He bellows, "Troy!"

A tall, thin teenager saunters out of the house. Cowboy hat and boots: black. Jeans and shirt: black. No tats showing.

Then I notice something shiny on the cowboy's collar. The word "hope" is printed in tiny rhinestones. He nods toward me and tells Bob, "You've frightened her."

Bob lumbers to his feet and tucks the bald flower behind my mom's ear. "Come on in."

Suddenly, the Subaru feels safe. My mom's track record for judging character leaves her at the back of the pack, every time. At least now I'm stranded in the car with food.

In six strides, Troy is at my side. He bends down and peers in. "His looks are worse than his bite."

"Sorry, not into vampires."

"Shapeshifters?"

I am trying not to be taken in by his gentle teasing. I am losing.

His smile flashes brighter than his hope pin as he glances at my hand. "Cool tat."

"Thanks."

Dark blue eyes rimmed in black, short, neat ponytail – the fear factor is diminishing. Besides, I have to go pee.

He opens the door. "Iced tea?"

My toe touches the driveway, warm but not too hot. "Look she's only here for some weed. It won't take long."

"You don't know my dad."

Troy is right.

We sit at a fifties era table in a kitchen so yellow it would probably smell like sunshine if it wasn't for the smoke. I listen to Bob and my mom tell sex, drugs, and rock-and-roll stories while they roll joints and get high.

My stomach tightens with a longing for knowledge. I am thirsty for family history, but not this. Not this.

Troy grabs a sandwich from the fridge and walks away, avoiding the smoke fest and missing most of the memories.

I head out to the car and grab some food from the cooler, along with the purple picnic blanket. Settling myself under a sycamore, I lean my back against its camouflage trunk. A strip of buffalo jerky is salty-sweet on my tongue.

The hours pass, even though it's now ninety degrees in the shade, I'd rather be outside than in the air-conditioned house. I take the pad and pencils out of my backpack, sketching leaf patterns and flowers.

The hours pass slow as the occasional insect that crawls across my drawing. I imagine pressing a tattoo machine against the thin skin on the top of a teenager's foot until a ladybug appears there. Or a giant mosquito on the bicep of a gangsta with the words "blood sucka!"

We stay for dinner. Pizza. My stomach clenches at the smell of garlic, visions of Oyster slime across my mind.

My mom hasn't bothered to mention my allergies. She and Bob are too caught up reminiscing about past adventures. Like the time a trap door opened in the middle of a song and swallowed the bass guitarist. And no one noticed until the concert ended.

"Mom, it's time to go." She has wasted our entire day.

The slice of pizza in her hand bobbles and she waves me away. Wasted.

I curl up on the couch with my sleeping bag, Grammie Rose's quilt, and my book, *The Blue Girl*. Maybe I'll finish it before I fall asleep. At least I don't have to worry about a gearshift poking me in the back.

Heavy breathing interrupts my reading. I ignore it for another sentence. At home, the yurt is small and I am used to grunts and groans.

But there is something warm and damp by my fingers. I rest the book on my chest and an enormous, slobbering, fanged face is staring at me. "Get away!"

Troy stands in the doorway laughing. At me. "Maybe Rosie likes your tat."

The beast turns its head toward him, but stands its ground. Troy squats down holding out his hand. "Rosebud. Come here, girl."

It trots over to him. He wraps his arms around it. "She's a bulldog. Sweet and beautiful."

"If that's your idea of beauty, I'd hate to see your girlfriend."

He kisses the smashed-in nose. "So that's why I don't have one!"

Disgusted, I go back to my reading. Does this count as improvisation or adaptation, Uncle Miles?

The morning is clear and cool. I pull the gold U of O Ducks sweatshirt out of my backpack and wriggle into it. My mom is pouring a mug of kombucha for Bob from her jar on the counter.

Breakfast is leftover pizza, left out all night. Possibly licked by the beast.

My mother stands by the sink washing her mug with Bob's giant paw resting on her backside. Stale smoke, garlic, and dog vie for the top smell of the morning.

If only I was enjoying an espresso with Amber on the Champs-Elysees.

Troy comes down the hall with a backpack and grins at me. "Adventure ready."

Star squeezes Bob's hand. "Load up, Rainbeau. Troy can have the back seat."

Troy?

"He's coming with us?" I ask, queen of the obvious.

Bob turns his shagginess toward me. I retreat, my arms full of sleeping bag and comforter and backpack.

He throws his arm around Troy's shoulders and Troy leans into the hug. "I'm due in Las Vegas tonight for a three-month gig. Sixteen's too young to spend that time alone. So your mom's dropping him off with his aunt in Chicago."

Troy picks up Rosie and tells her, "You'll be spoiled by the old wrinkled one across the street.

His dad says, "Works for everyone."

My mom hugs the giant jar. "Good news! Oyster is going to meet us in the Windy City and we can spend a couple of days with him!"

My stomach stiffens and maggots crawl through the cornrows across my scalp.

Troy hikes his bag on his shoulder, his eyebrow raised. "Oyster?"

"My mom's manfriend." I rake my nails through my braids. "She dug him out of the muck."

Star is busy kissing Bob goodbye. Either she didn't hear me or, more likely, she doesn't care what I think.

We clamber into the car. The scoby rests on the floor by Troy's feet.

Headed out of town we pass a giant rock with a horseshoe shaped sign, "Gateway to the Northwest". We head toward the highway, away from the sign, away from Oregon, away from home.

Six

Troy stretches out on the recently emptied back seat. "Here's a story even you'll love, Miss Dog Despiser."

I am thankful for one thing. The drooling mess went to a neighbor's. "Slobber and slime and a face that looks like it ran into a truck. Can't wait."

No comment. Great. Now I'm on my way to Utah with two people who ignore me.

My mother in her best suck-up voice says, "I want to hear the story."

He flashes an I-recognize-that-voice-but-I'll-be-polite smile. "One time, I gave Rosie bologna. When my dad walked into the kitchen, a thin piece of the casing was hanging out of her mouth. He was convinced it was the tail of a mouse, still half-alive, so he tried to pry her jaws apart. Not easy with a bulldog."

Star is doing her snorting laugh. "Did he succeed?"

"No. She swallowed it and licked her lips. I had to tell him it was bologna before he burst into tears. He's such a softy."

The second positive: Troy is more entertaining than my mom.

As if on cue, but not on key, my mom sings, "We're going to the Church of Jesus Christ of Latter Day Saints!"

A thought floats through my mind and lands in my stomach like a lead balloon. "Mom, are you a Mormon?"

She shakes her head and changes the tune. "Oh, when we go marching in to the Church of Jesus Christ of Latter Day Saints!"

A sigh whistles through my lips.

My mother, the spirituality addict: Buddha, yoga, LSD, LDS, whatever.

The gas gauge is below a quarter of a tank when we reach Wells, Nevada. "Mom, we need to stop."

She pulls into the first station we see. "I'll be right back." She walks away, her Birkenstocks slapping the hot pavement.

The only thing I don't know about cars, besides driving, is how to pump gas. In Oregon, only the people who work at the station are allowed that privilege. "Can you fill it?" I ask Troy as I get out of the car.

He unfolds his long legs from the back seat. "Sure."

I walk into a blast of burnt coffee and nasty hot dogs in the QuickieMart and check to see if my mom has paid. I don't see her, so she must be in the bathroom. A burly man with a spider web tattooed on his neck sniffs the air and asks the clerk, "Do you smell skunk, Harvey?"

The man behind the counter answers, "No, but I see one in the store."

Did he see a real skunk or smell marijuana on my mom? Fear bristles up my spine, chased by confusion. One thing I do know, the tat means he's been in prison and considers himself a fly caught in the government's web.

We are out of here. Oyster's money comes in handy. It's not worth waiting for the change.

My mom leaves the restroom wiping her hands on her skirt and I grab her arm. "Let's go." Steering her out of the store, my grip on her elbow is Rosie-the-bulldog strong.

She tries to shake me off. "What's the problem?"

"You!" I shout. Head down, hoping the men won't confront us, I hustle her to the car.

There are so many possibilities for disaster with Star that an earthquake would be a relief.

Back on the road, we're rolling along and my mom says, "Don't you think it's interesting that some guy in the eighteen hundreds calls himself a prophet, marries a bunch of women, has a gazillion kids, and gets thousands of people to follow him out to the desert?"

I stop picking at the thread on my jeans. "Why would anyone follow him? Are some people just born leaders?"

Troy leans forward in the back seat. "Or do they learn it?"

My mom is quiet for a long moment. "Maybe it's both. Someone could be born with a strong will, but they'd have to learn how to be wise. Siddhartha was a prince, but he had to leave the palace for the wilderness and learn wisdom to become the Buddha."

I face Troy to see what he will say.

He holds up the Buddha/toad that was sitting on the back

seat and wiggles it at me. "Hitler wasn't wise, but he was a leader."

My mom asks, "Remember Siddhartha's fight with the demons?"

With my finger on my jeans I trace two figure eights in the shape of a cross. "Like the devil tempting Jesus in the desert?"

Star's chin bounces up and down like a bobble-headed doll on the dash of a vintage Volvo. "They chose the path of good: enlightenment."

Troy rubs his finger across the rhinestones on his collar. "Hitler chose the dark path."

I hesitate, my heart beating hard enough to hurt. "How do we know if we're on the right path?"

"Intuition," my mom replies. "Even if it's difficult or scary, it feels right."

It sounds so easy.

Could intuition be mistaken? Could decisions that were made for you be good or bad? Could a path seem right to the chooser and wrong to everyone else?

If only I had answers instead of questions. But I don't ask my mom. She may be on the path to enlightenment, but I'm not sure if she's ahead of me or behind.

We are quiet for the next hour until we drive into Salt Lake City where flocks of seagulls hover over the lake.

I'm tempted to sketch them. "Why are there ocean birds in Utah?"

"Not sure," Troy says. "But there is a story. Brigham Young and his followers planted crops when they arrived here. A swarm of katydids descended and began devouring the harvest. The gulls flew in and decimated the pests. The Mormons call it the miracle of the gulls."

Troy guides us to the Temple Square. "We used to visit Salt Lake City when my dad dated a Mormon."

My mom slides the Subaru into a sunny spot in the middle of a gigantic parking lot. Signs direct us to the South Visitors' Center.

We stand at the back of a crowd while a guide shows a video on the history of the church.

A man with a lime green t-shirt reading 'I'm with stupid', asks, "What about all the wives? Where can I get me a couple extra?"

The woman next to him, who is wearing a matching shirt, punches him on the arm. "How 'bout some more husbands? Or maybe I could just trade this one in."

The docent makes an obvious effort not to roll her eyes. "I'm glad you mentioned that. The church officially abandoned polygamy in 1890. Polyandry was never a common practice. Besides, would you really want an extra husband?"

When the laughter fades, she adds, "Family is fundamental to the church. The vows a couple takes are not just for this life, but for all eternity."

Troy curls his forefingers and locks them together, pulling and grimacing. I glance away, wanting to laugh. But my heart gives a little twist and I wonder what it would be like if family was forever. I guess it would depend on the family.

The guide leads the group out to the square. A thin man with a faded mass of green on his bicep asks a question. But instead of listening, I am thinking Miles could cover up that mess with a decent tattoo. Someday I'll replace ugly with beautiful, too.

Troy is cleaning his fingernails with his knife. People around him notice and step away.

My mom bounces with excitement in her hot pink Wymyn First! t-shirt. She's sure to make an impression. I don't understand her enthusiasm for learning about religion.

Troy crooks his finger beckoning me to follow. He lights a hand-rolled cigarette, takes a few puffs, and hands it to me.

My shoulders relax when I smell tobacco. "No thanks. Are you sure that's okay to do here?"

"Who cares what these uptight idiots think?"

"They're just different, that's all." Wait. Why am I defending the Mormons?

He blows smoke over my head. "You're not one of them. What do you care?"

"How well do you know me? Maybe the tourist crowds are infiltrated by Mormon teens, experts in conversion." I try to keep my dimple from betraying me.

He laughs until he coughs and crushes the cigarette under the heel of his black cowboy boot. "I'll buy you a coffee. You drink, don't you?"

"Is that a trick question to see if I'm really a Mormon?"

He throws his hands up in mock horror. "Maybe you are a spy!"

I glance toward my mom who is surrounded by the group as they disappear around a corner. I'm certain she will not miss us.

Troy strides out of the square and down the street. Three blocks later, he opens a door between a cobbler and a dry cleaner. I am wondering how well I know him. The street is empty. Hesitating on the threshold, I hear a creak, creak, creak. A small sign, painted with a steaming mug and the words "Common Grounds" swings above my head. The smell of coffee wafts down the stairs and I follow Troy up.

Half of the old building's second floor is a coffee shop. Ancient sagging couches and stuffed chairs, faded to gray, line the walls by the windows.

I head for the "Help Yourself" sign, checking for soy or rice milk. I settle for stuffing a handful of sugar packets in my pocket and then grab a few more.

Troy carries two small coffees and places them on a round wooden table in the corner.

"Thanks!" I slide into a chair so I can watch the entrance.

He pulls the other seat around so he's facing the stairs, too. After taking a sip from his speckled gray mug, he wraps his hand around his chin and taps his lips with his finger. "Rainbeau. Rain from the land of rain."

How observant.

I could grind beans between my clenched teeth. Why do people insist on shortening Rainbeau? Is it that hard to add the extra syllable?

I open four packets of sugar and the white crystals dance into my mug. Thoughts of sparkling tattoo inks tap around my brain.

"So where are you headed?" He lights a cigarette in spite of the fact that we are sitting under a "No Smoking!" sign.

"There's a BFA program at the U of O. If I go there, I can apprentice at the shop. Eventually, I'll want my own place, so I'll need to find somewhere the market isn't so saturated."

Head slightly turned, he sucks on his cigarette and blows a smoke ring. "Market saturated? U of O? BFA? I thought you were going to grandma's. Which is where?"

"Oh." I fold the empty sugar packets into tiny fans, trying to decide if his blue eyes are piercing or compassionate. "We are. Massachusetts."

"And the letter list?"

"Bachelor of Fine Arts at the University of Oregon. Tattoo artists have BFAs now, but there are too many of them in Eugene."

A smoke ring wobbles past my chin. "A degree in tattooing?"

"No. I wish. You study art and still have to apprentice. Ink in skin isn't the same as ink on paper."

Up the stairs comes greasy hair, a Vandyke beard, a tweed jacket. How did he find me? I'm gripping the mug hard enough to crack the handle. I spill the coffee, burning my shaking hands.

Troy jumps out of his chair, patting me with napkins.

I cannot move. I cannot think. I cannot breathe.

Oyster turns toward us. It is not Oyster. The face is older, thinner, kinder.

"Little Beau, are you okay?"

Little Beau is way worse than Rain. Besides, what should I tell him? That the guy who walked up the stairs looks like my mom's manfriend, who I stole hundreds of dollars from? Who tried to rape me?

"Fine, T." So much simpler.

He sits back in his chair, nodding. "T's chill."

As the blood pumps through my veins again, my hand throbs where I spilled the super hot coffee.

Troy takes a sip and I wonder if he lacks nerve endings in his lips or is too cool to acknowledge pain.

Maybe he's cool and tough. And I am neither.

We talk about books as he finishes his coffee, then head back to the visitor's center.

My mom is so animated after the tour, I am wondering if they handed out happy pills. "Family is forever!" she exclaims.

"Mom, you didn't sign up or anything, did you?"

"Religion is like kombucha tea. You fill yourself up when parched."

That doesn't really answer the question.

We are five feet away from the Subaru when we smack into a worse than skunks-and-rotting-garbage-and-outhouses-when-you're-camping smell.

Troy backs up a few paces to the no-stink zone. But my mom races to the car, screaming.

With my hand covering my mouth and nose, I brave the foul odor.

She flings open the door to the sun-heated car. "My baby!"

"My baby" is her tea. "My baby" is not me.

Troy runs forward, followed by a small group of strangers. A woman in a beige business suit whips out a cell phone and begins dialing.

Mortified, I shout, "Stop!"

The woman blinks, but doesn't push any more buttons.

Star is cradling the gallon jar in her arms, sobbing like a normal person would if they had lost a child. She squats on her heels, rocking.

"Mom, it's a friggin' mushroom!"

Tears run down her face. "How can you say that!" She wails clutching the jar, seemingly immune to the horrible stench.

People are staring. I do not want to deal with this. I want to push my way through the crowd and disappear. Get myself adopted by a Mormon family.

The woman begins dialing again. I throw Troy a desperate glance. He looks like an enormous raven, spreading his wings wide and moving the crowd. They amble away, shaking their heads at the hysterical woman crying over what looks like a giant jar of iced tea.

Troy focuses on the woman in beige. His arm around her shoulder, she nods and I wonder what he has said. Maybe he told her we're taking mom to the looney bin. Maybe we should.

I try to get her in the car, but she won't budge.

Troy kneels by my mom, his hand on her back, reassuring her. "You can have a goodbye ceremony at the lake."

She nods and crawls into the back seat, the jar on her lap.

I roll down the windows, hoping we don't have far to go. Breathing through my mouth allows the putrid smell to crawl down my throat faster. If I was taller, I could hang my head out the window like Amber's Miniature Pinschers when they sit on her lap.

Troy drives us to a quiet park by the lake. He grabs his tobacco pouch and we get out of the car.

He leads my mom toward the water, while I trail behind. She rambles on about how good the scoby has been to her. "I haven't been sick in seven years, because of you." She begins to bawl again. "How could I have left you in that oven of a car!"

At the edge of the water, Troy unwinds the leather strip

from around the button on his tobacco pouch.

Tipping the jar, my mother murmurs, "Goodbye, dear scoby." It slides into the salty water. She sprinkles a few grains of tobacco. Leaving the glass container by the water's edge, she trudges toward the Subaru.

Troy leans over and whispers, "Do kombuchas go to heaven?"

Relief seeps through me with the laughter. He may not be an adult, but he's dealing with my mom's drama. "Let's hope it doesn't reappear."

"Giant scoby spotted on Great Salt Lake."

Laughter at the absurdity of Star, of kombucha, of my life loosens my tension-tightened muscles. "Thanks for helping with the crowd back there."

"No problem. It was like herding the doggies on my uncle's ranch. Without the horse."

Troy picks up the jar and sets it next to a nearby trashcan. I search for some fragrant flower or herb that will dispel the awful smell in the car.

When I come back with a handful of pine needles, my mom is sitting under a tree, asleep. The faint odor of marijuana is mixed in with the scent of dead scoby. I scatter the needles throughout the car, doubting they will help.

Troy is relaxing on a bench, watching seagulls fight over the pieces of bread he is throwing in the air. They whiz by his head and he doesn't cringe.

I stand back, worried that he is feeding them my gluten-free millet bread, but too scared to approach. The gathering of gulls shrieks loudly over the last few crusts.

When they are gone, I plop down next to Troy. The bag in his hand is a brand I don't recognize. "Let me guess, she's high."

"Yup."

"Are you?" I hold my breath, hoping he isn't. There is no way I can handle one stupefied adult and one stupid teenager.

"Nope."

Air fills my lungs, clean air, air that doesn't reek. I wrap my arms around my shins, chin resting on my knees. We sit quietly together. In the distance, the birds harangue a couple who are walking down the beach holding a box of crackers.

Troy has saved a large crumb for a hesitant chipmunk. Troy is definitely one of the good guys.

I stare at the huge lake, tiny ripples washing along the shore. Wondering what is God's plan in all of this? Wishing I knew, so I wouldn't feel like a piece of bread tossed in the air.

My mother has left me stranded. Again.

There's no time for self pity, I need to be practical. "Will you drive?"

Troy takes the keys out of his pocket and we walk toward the car. When his hand rests on my shoulder, I don't even flinch.

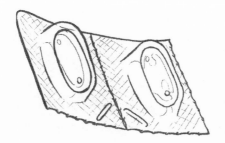

Seven

Troy drives the Subaru, even pressure on the gas pedal, seventy-five miles an hour. We like the same loud music on the radio. And he doesn't sing.

My mom is the quintessence of quiet. Quintessence. The ultimate word I learned from Amber. Where is she now? Milan? Vienna? She won't even be able to send me postcards, because I didn't give her my grandmother's address. I hug Grammie Rose's quilt, but it isn't as comforting as an Amber hug.

My stomach gurgles, but eating another protein bar is as appealing as drinking kombucha before the big stink.

Hunger pangs burble, clench, ouch. "Mom, can I have a piece of fruit from the cooler?"

When she doesn't answer, I turn around, slipping out of the shoulder belt.

She is asleep – sprawled on the back seat surrounded by

wrappers and rinds. In the cooler, nestled among the ice, is a lone cherry tomato.

"Stop!" I yell. "How far are we from the city?"

Troy doesn't even take his foot off the gas. "Whoa, Little Beau! What's the problem?"

I accent each word as if he has the I.Q. of a turnip, "My mom ate all our food."

"Yup. One hell of a case of the munchies."

"You saw her!" I punch him on the arm. "Why didn't you say something?"

Troy wrenches the wheel and we are on the side of the highway. He opens his door. "Get out."

The hair on my arms salutes the fireworks in my intestines. He can't really leave me here, can he? My mom hasn't even woken up. How long would it take her to notice I was gone?

We both climb out of the Subaru. Troy leans against the hood and lights a cigarette. Stabbing the air in my direction, punctuating his demand. "You will not hit me." He sucks on the cigarette and the tip glows.

My muscles harden waiting for a fight or flight message from my brain. The third option: possum. Except I don't think he'll believe me if I pretend to drop dead.

He turns his head blowing the smoke away from my face. Tension radiates off him, defensive not offensive. "I will not hit you or your mom."

I stare at Amber's decorations on my sneakers, swirls and stars and squiggles. "I'm sorry. Really." I chance a look into the blue of his eyes, more cobalt than sky, surprised that he is smiling.

"What's up with the food freak-out, Little…"

"Don't call me that." I stick my hands into the pockets of my jeans. "I don't like it."

"Ohhhhkay." He waits.

It's one of his talents, like managing Star so I can be fourteen instead of forty. "I was handling things just fine before you came along." I'm thankful he's here and all I can do is say something stupid. Why can't I tell him how I feel?

The anger in his eyes is gone and all I see in them is concern. He blows a series of smoke rings.

I turn my head to avoid the smell of tobacco. "There's stuff you don't know."

The understatement of understatements.

The words, "I have food allergies," come out in a breathy rush.

"Hives?"

"No. Anaphylactic – deadly."

He stamps out his cigarette. "The freak-out."

He eases behind the steering wheel, so I plop into the passenger seat. When he doesn't ask, I launch into the list "Nuts, gluten, dairy, beef, chicken, turkey, and shellfish." Steeling myself for the usual comeback, "what do you eat?"

Instead, he turns the key in the ignition, looks in both directions, and pulls a U-turn. "I saw a sign for a health food store about ten miles back."

I rub my eyes, trying to get rid of that pre-tears prickly feeling. Why does kindness make me want to cry? If only his understanding extended to Oyster, because I am definitely allergic to shellfish. But there is no way could I tell him. What if he thought the Oyster attack was my fault? What if it was?

We don't bother to wake Star when we arrive. I rifle through her fanny pack searching for cash. She's hidden some money in her "secret" place, the packaging of a menstrual pad.

In the store, Troy chases me with the cart. I jump on and he wheels me down the aisles. We giggle like a pair of kids with a pickle. While he juggles pears, I bag peaches.

At the register, the clerk has an anarchist tattoo, an "A" in a circle, on his wrist. His glazed glance fixes on the food and he looks more into de-evolution than revolution.

I slide a bar of chocolate up my sleeve, guessing I won't have enough cash to buy it, saving the Oyster money for emergencies.

Troy grabs my hand. I startle and squeal, my heart beating faster than a racing grocery cart. He whispers in my ear, "I'll pay for that," slips the bar out and places it on the conveyor belt. Then he throws a Wyoming guidebook on top. I pony up Star's cash and Troy kicks in the extra.

We load the Subaru, his face a study in frowns. "You shouldn't steal."

"You shouldn't smoke." But the truth is I'm trembling – I've never been caught before.

"I won't go to jail for smoking."

"Only to the hospital or the morgue."

We climb into the car. Troy doesn't respond, but the stiffness in his shoulders and the absence of his smile tell me all I need to know. Stealing a candy bar was never a big deal before. But now, now I'm ashamed.

I reach out and rest my fingertips, light as mist, on his arm. "I'm sorry. Thanks for buying it."

He takes his hand off the wheel and pats my thigh. Shock waves roll up my leg and suddenly it's hard to breathe, but this time I can't blame the allergies.

Star wakes up with a groan. "Ugh, my stomach!" She is too stuffed to eat anything for dinner.

Troy munches the sandwich he bought and I devour half a bag of baby carrots and some salmon jerky. We share the chocolate for dessert.

With Troy driving, the landscape whizzes by. We pass a scraped and scarred white pick-up chugging along on the two-lane highway. An eighteen-wheeler barrels toward us. My fingers dig into the faux leather of the seat. If my nails were longer, there would be ten half-moon punctures. He calmly maneuvers the Subaru into the lane and winks at me.

It's been almost three hours since we left Salt Lake City. We stop to fill the gas tank and use the restrooms in Rock Springs, Wyoming. I see a sign for a town named Reliance. Reliance, Paisley — my mom's kind of towns. She must have taken some pills because she's passed out, again.

Troy keeps driving and I relax into the peaceful quiet. Sketchbook on my lap, I doodle tribal bands until I feel like I've turned the color of an asparagus. Carsick sucks.

I look out the window and wonder where we'll find a motel.

Twilight settles, the first star twinkling in the East.

Troy says, "Time to set up camp." He pulls over on the side of the road, somewhere in Wyoming. No town, no lights, just highway and hills, bulls and barbed wire.

"The cow pasture looks comfortable," he teases.

Camping is fine with me. I haul my pup tent out of the back

of the car. Five minutes later it's set up. "Where are you going to sleep?"

His belongings are scattered on the ground. T-shirts, boxers, and black jeans rolled up beside a pair of socks and a water bottle. "I thought I brought my sleeping bag. Wrong again."

Star is still sprawled on the back seat, snoring. The purple picnic blanket wrapped around her, dotted with chunks and crumbs.

I toss him my mom's sleeping bag. "Good night."

He pulls it around him, his hat covering his face on one end and cowboy boots sticking out the other. "Sleep tight. Don't let the bed bugs bite." He slaps at a mosquito.

They are vicious. I crawl into my tent zipping the flap in a flash.

I lie on top of my sleeping bag and write Miles an imaginary postcard. "In a field in Wyoming. The cows moo, 'Hello!' Wish you were here."

The sun is up at a quarter to six and we are on the road fifteen minutes later. Troy zooms down the highway, chasing the rising fireball. He slips on his sunglasses without hitting the brakes.

The Pacific side of Oregon was all greens and blues. Wyoming is reds and yellows: ketchup and mustard colored mountains.

I am definitely hungry.

We speed toward Nebraska and eat breakfast out of the cooler, not bothering to stop. It's only Tuesday and I feel like I've spent six years in the Subaru. But now that Troy is with us, life with my mom isn't so miserable.

He lets up on the gas pedal and we are traveling at the speed limit. We pass a patrol car hidden behind some bushes. "Just had a feeling."

When we are out of range, he takes us back to seventy-five.

My mom would never have noticed the trap. Of course, she would have been going thirty miles an hour slower. Do they give tickets for driving too slow?

I turn around and watch her weave a batch of bracelets. She twists red, white, and royal blue strands together, pointing her chin at the guidebook. "Why don't you see what it says about Wyoming?"

On the cover is a cowboy in a huge hat sitting on a brown and white spotted horse. What kind of crazy person would get on such a huge animal?

I thumb through the pages and find a section highlighted in pink. "Did you know that Wyoming was the first state, well, territory, to let women vote in 1870?"

My audience seems suitably impressed.

"Wyoming also had the first woman judge, Esther Morris. She helped pass the law allowing women to vote."

Even the guidebook doesn't keep us occupied for long. There's nothing but static on the radio. Troy's whistling is the only thing preventing me from falling asleep. It's a tune I've never heard before and each time he repeats it, he changes it just a little.

Five hours later we roll into a gas station in Ogallala, Nebraska, on fumes.

"Here," my mom shoves the bracelets she's been making into my hands. "See if you can sell these at the tourist shop.

Remember to tell them you're an Indian."

As I walk away, I hear her say, "It'd be an easier sell if she didn't have her hair in corn rows."

Why doesn't she think a town named Ogallala has its own Native Americans?

Besides, I hate to sell anything except tattoos.

Stepping into the darkness of a shop, I wait for my eyes to adjust. The first thing I see is a woman in a flowered hat brushing by the fake plastic scalps hanging from a pillar. A man is taking photos of a wooden Indian that I'd bet was made in China.

"Over here!" The woman screams, waddling in my direction.

Ducking around a display of tomahawks painted with popular children's names one of my braids catches on an "Elizabeth."

"That is precisely what I'm looking for!"

A racially mixed fourteen-year-old?

Her hat fans my face and she grabs the bracelets. "Where did you buy these?"

"My mom made them."

The woman turns, quite a feat for a large person in the small aisle, yelling, "Derrick!" When he appears, she says, "Aren't these exactly what I was hoping to find here?"

He examines the turquoise and tangerine bracelet. "They're well-made. Do you work here?"

I shake my head. "No."

He herds us outside like a border collie with two errant geese. "Well, now we can talk business. How much do you want?"

I ask for twice as much money as my mom usually gets.

"Why there are enough for all the women in the garden club. I must have them."

Derrick hesitates and offers less.

I try to sound carefree, hoping my voice won't squeak, "No thanks." I force myself to turn away.

The woman swats her husband with her pocketbook.

He reaches into his wallet. "Oh, all right." And pulls out the bills, new and crisp and green. "Sold."

The woman squeals and smacks her husband – with a kiss.

I walk back to the car, shoving half the money in my pocket. Two bills curled tightly in my fist to give my mom.

I head up Front Street past the jail and the tonsorial palace. Is that really what they call barber shops out here?

When I get to the café, Mom and Troy are already seated.

Star holds out her hand for the money. "Time for lunch!"

"Not even a thanks?"

She stuffs the bills in her fanny pack. "Sure. Thanks."

It's noon, but the place looks like a ghost town the day after Halloween. The cleanser smell doesn't hide the odor of stale grease. We settle into a booth, the crimson naugahyde benches creaking. A waitress, older than my mom and hair piled high, brings us menus, filling our coffee mugs to the brim.

Beef, chicken, and one shrimp dish. No pork, no lamb, no tofu. The only thing buffalo on the menu is wings. Isn't this the Great Plains?

My mom and Troy take forever to decide what to have. I guess that's what happens when you have choices. "Mom, nothing's organic."

She closes her menu. "When in Ogallala, do what the Ogallalans do."

We wait for the waitress and my chest begins to contract. Each slow, even breath an effort. "I'll be right back," I whisper.

In the bathroom, I lean my head against the stall door, below the broken coat hook. Am I just anxious about being in the diner or are there enough molecules in the air to cause an allergic reaction?

My throat is tight. Is my tongue swelling? My lungs ache. I wait for the bathroom door to swing open, desperately wanting my mom to check on me.

Inhale. Exale. I can still breathe, so I head back to the table.

Troy slams his mug down hard enough for the coffee to slosh over the side. "You can't eat lunch while she's sitting there with nothing!"

My mom takes a napkin from the dispenser. "She can get something to eat from the car!" She tears the paper in two. "You don't need to worry about her. She can take care of herself."

Troy sops up the spilled coffee. "How do you think she feels?"

Will they ask me?

"She's used to it!" Star turns toward me. "Aren't you?"

"Yes," I answer without thinking, but it's true.

Troy taps his spoon on the table. "That does not make it okay."

My mom and her friends do this to me. A lot. Why is he the one that cares?

"I don't even know what 'normal' food tastes like." My voice is tomahawk sharp. "So what difference does it make?"

His "hope" pin glitters in the sunshine, but it is the hurt in his eyes that cuts through me. I sit on the bench, hands tucked under my thighs, staring at the fly buzzing the pie on the counter.

The waitress, in a stained steel blue uniform, returns, pen poised to take our order. On her wrist is a tattoo that says, " Type 1 Diabetes".

Troy tells her, "I'll have a burger and fries and a sasparilla, please."

My mom adds, "A bowl of vegetable soup."

The waitress looks at me and I shake my head.

The tip of my nose and my lips are tingling. Focusing inward, I try to untangle my feelings from my symptoms— the knot too complex to release.

Troy rests his hand on my arm, running his thumb along the hairs there. "Are you okay?"

"Yeah, I'll go hang out in the car." I stand and catch his frowning, head tilted, look of concern.

My mom says, "She'll be fine."

Is the power of her intention stronger than allergens, stronger than reactions, stronger than death?

Eight

I am finally awake, curled up on the back seat with Grammie's quilt wrapped warm and soft around me. Troy's sweater is a pillow smelling of soap and sweat and cigarettes. I breathe deep and my muscles relax. The fear of dying fades.

Star pulls into a gas station. "Iowa. Time to fill the tank."

A giant lemon yellow water tower with a smiley face looms over me. I should wonder what time it is. I should have to go pee. I should be hungry, but all I want is water.

Across the street is a blinking "Longview Mote" sign lighting up the twilight sky. After paying for gas, Star drives over and parks beneath it. "Wake up, sleepy head. It's time for bed!" She laughs like she'll win the award for funniest mom in the world.

I follow her into the office, lugging my backpack. She pays for two rooms and I notice the breath I've been holding is back to normal. Camping out is one thing, sharing a hotel room with

Troy is another. Thankfully, even my mom won't stoop to that level of inappropriateness.

Outside, Troy's fingers are laced through a chain link fence. He is gazing at a small, clean, rectangular pool. He follows us, whistling the tune from Psycho.

The rooms smell like bleach with hints of mold. The orange and brown bedspread belongs in a Hitchcock film. I reach for my sketchbook, determined to draw the geometric pattern.

Troy opens the door between our rooms. "Hey, Beau, can I see your artwork?"

My mother never asks to see my flash.

I step into his room and hand him my sketchbook. "Some are still pretty rough."

He flips past an LDS saint covered in tribal, the leaves and insects of Winnemucca, the Chihuahua clown from Lakeview, and stops at the picture of the rainbow yin-yang with the three snakes border. "Wow! This is really good."

"Um, thanks. They'd be better if I had a full set of rapidograph pens." He's staring at the drawing and I am wondering what he's thinking, arguing with myself about whether or not I should ask. He hands it back without another word.

Collapsing in a backward dive onto the queen-sized bed, he says, "Want to go for a swim?"

"Sure!"

My pack, with the bathing suit buried at the bottom, is in the room I'm sharing with my mom. Amber always says to keep one handy, because you never know.

I wiggle into last year's tankini, three inches of brown belly proof that I've grown. The top is tight, too, but it's not like I have any cleavage.

"We're going swimming," I tell my mom. She digs through her suitcase. I'm about to ask if she's coming, when I realize I don't want her in the pool. "Remember, no smoking in the room!"

Troy's suit covers most of his thighs. His muscular calves are covered with dark hair. Barefoot, I trot ahead. He follows, picking his way across the gravel. An image of the curve of his lips flashes through my mind.

When we get to the pool, I notice the tip of a tattoo peeking over his shorts. My bikini bottom feels way too tight and I am certain Troy is not sibling material.

We are alone. I dip my toes in the cool water and read all the rules. He dives off the deep end breaking number three and swims the entire length underwater before surfacing.

He splashes me and the water sparkles, diamonds against a grungy parking lot background. I kick until foam surrounds me, a giant bubble bath. Throughly soaked, I slip into the pool.

The water supports me, comforts me, envelopes me. Evening is my favorite time to float, looking up at the azure sky. My legs hang down and my belly gently rises with each breath. Long minutes, calm minutes pass.

Forever time: if only the world would stop, freeze forever. The feeling of oneness from the waterfall returns. Is this what it is like to be with God?

Troy ripples the surface, swimming slow, languorous laps. He passes me and his fingertips brush my shoulder.

I am electrified. My nipples harden and I roll over in the

water and breaststroke to the edge. My back turned toward him, I step out of the pool, wrapping a towel tightly around my torso.

When he climbs out, I throw a towel at him, barely missing his head. I rush back to the room and he tries to keep up, groaning over the gravel. "Why the rush, Beau?"

My face is flushed. I squeeze my arms across my chest, my nipples still hard. Flustered, I mumble something incoherent.

Neither of us thought to bring a key. I bang on the door and ignore his curious glances. When my mom lets us in, a way-too-familiar musky smell wafts out.

"Mom! You promised."

"I did not." She waves her hand in Troy's direction. "Nice tat."

He crosses the threshold and pulls his suit down millimeter by millimeter. My gaze is locked on the space below his navel.

"Thor's hammer," he says, stopping.

Too early or just in time?

Troy adds, "It's a Norse thing."

And, my mother asks, "Do you have any others?"

Quivering with curiosity, I do not wait for his reply. I am too afraid that he will notice the heat rising off me, pool water turned to steam.

I hurry to the bathroom, peel off my wet suit, stand under the shower's hot, pelting drops. My mind drifts from Troy to tattoos to the familiar groove of designing my own shop.

A head-to-toe check reveals that my body is back to normal, thoughts of Troy's hammer banished. I throw on shorts and a tank top before leaving the bathroom.

They've placed an order for Chinese food. More forbidden food.

I go with Troy to pick up the take-out and try not think about his tat or his muscular calves. We walk the few blocks in silence. My skin tingles with the closeness of him. Sixteen…too old…sixteen…too old – reverbs through my brain.

He blows smoke rings at the giant neon sign, "Panda's Heaven". "I thought they only ate bamboo."

"Maybe that's all they serve: bamboo egg roll, bamboo chow mein, bamboo moo goo gai pan."

"If you can eat bamboo, you're all set."

I won't take a chance. The epipens in my backpack press up against my kidney a reminder of times I did.

We each carry a bag – Troy has the one with the shellfish. It leaks brown sauce down his pants. "There are worse things than smelling like lobster sauce!"

"Yeah, Oyster!"

Troy's left eyebrow rises in an unspoken question.

I want to tell him what happened, but I don't.

At the motel, my mom and Troy sit on his bed, open Chinese food containers surrounding them. She plucks an eggroll with her chopsticks. Troy shovels fried rice with a small plastic fork. In between mouthfuls, they argue about which movie to watch.

I wander around the room I'm sharing with my mom, munching a rice cake. There is no way I'll watch the vampire film they picked. Besides, they didn't ask my opinion.

My sketchbook is lying on the bed so I dig out my pencils and cover the page with a giant panda surrounded by bamboo. His round tummy and satisfied look make me smile. It's less angular than the one I drew for Amber, but she'd like this one, too.

I imagine tattooing a Panda on some giant guy's chest – eyes around the nipples, matching big bellies. How different does it feel to press the needles in where there's fat instead of muscle? I'll have to remember to ask Miles.

When I turn out the light, together my mom and Troy call, "Goodnight!"

I crawl between the scratchy sheets. Trying to ignore the sound of laughter from the next room and the pang of jealousy piercing my heart, I finally fall asleep.

In my dream, I am searching a dirty bathroom for a clean stall. I wake up needing to pee. The door between our room and Troy's is open and the television creates a ghostly glow. It's 4:34 a.m.

I stumble past my mom and Troy fast asleep.

In the bathroom, a thought hovers. I banish it, wrapping myself in the tatters of dreams.

On the way back to bed, it bursts through my brain in giant neon: my mom and Troy asleep together, snuggled close. My mother in a large t-shirt and underwear. The flickering light of the television reveals Troy's tight boxers hugging the muscles of his thighs.

My stomach clenches hard and it is definitely not undigested rice cake. The jeans and sweatshirt I'd left on the chair next to my bed aren't there. Where are my clothes?

A neat pile sits on the foot of my mother's bed. I rifle through them, scattering shirts and skirts and undies.

I am numb. It is better than the feeling of betrayal I am

78

fighting to suppress. I yank on a sweatshirt and jeans and head into the cool night without my backpack.

But outside, the soft air caresses my skin and an ache pulls me out of my stupor. Troy isn't my boyfriend. He's sixteen.

It doesn't help. He's way too young for my mother.

Crickets hum and stars twinkle. I walk and walk and walk.

I plunk down by a rock the size of the Subaru and the musty smell of damp earth fills the air.

Is this what it feels like when your heart breaks? I want to beat the stone with my fists and scream into the night. If the skies opened up in a downpour accompanied by thunder and lightning it wouldn't match my feelings. It would take a hurricane or a tornado. But the night is clear.

My wracking, wrenching breaths eventually turn into a whimper.

How could she sleep with Troy?

My mom always ruins everything.

I wake, back pressed against the rough rock. Wheels squeal and a cloud of dust hovers around the familiar green Subaru. My mother is driving. "Get in!"

I push myself up and rub the grit from my eyes. I see no need to rush.

"Hurry!" Troy yells.

What is up with Mr. Mellow? I thought you're supposed to feel relaxed after sex.

He leaps out of the car and jumps into the back seat, leaving the front door open. I climb in and Star peels away while I am still buckling. Lips compressed, eyes tight, faces grim, maybe they feel guilty.

7:52. The itch of curiosity trumps the rawness of my anger. "What's wrong?"

Star looks at Troy in the rearview mirror. His slight nod seems to give her permission to speak. "Bob was injured on the job this morning."

I turn and ask Troy. "How bad?"

He shakes his head. His hands tremble and he fumbles with a cigarette, but doesn't light it.

My mom answers, "He had a stroke and fell." She is driving beyond the speed limit. "Troy is flying home. He'd have been on his way by now if you hadn't disappeared."

Troy's eyes are liquid pools, his voice hoarse, "Please, don't argue."

In silence we race toward Des Moines. Closer to Chicago, closer to Oyster.

Red rage, slate sadness, drab despair, and a tiny thread of golden guilt whirl into a ball of emotion too tough to untangle.

An hour later, we are at the airport and Troy rushes toward the airline employee behind the desk. "I have to get on the next plane to Vegas!"

The woman, wearing a nametag that identifies her as "friendly and cheerful", keeps typing.

Troy waits about three seconds. "It's an emergency!"

Her words clipped and precise, she mentions a huge sum for the flight.

"I don't have that kind of money!" Neither does my mom.

The employee's cheek twitches and her eyes narrow. "Do you have a credit card?"

My mom shrugs. Troy begins to collapse, first his head, then his shoulders, then his waist. A tear falls. A dark splotch on the charcoal fabric of his backpack.

I want to be mad at him, but that one drop washes the feeling away and all that's left is sorry.

I pull the balled-up wad of Oyster's cash out of my pocket and hand it to him.

"Rainbeau," my mom says, her face clouded with concern, "Where did you get that?"

My gaze is locked on the tear stain. "My flash."

Troy's fingers rub the blue-violet bead on one of my braids. "Thank you, Beau."

The money lays on the counter and the woman eyes the crumpled bills with obvious distaste.

It is all the Oyster stash, all the bracelet money, all I have.

It is enough. He gets his ticket.

When we explain the situation, the woman security officer lets us wait with him at the gate. His flight is announced and he gives my mother a huge hug.

Anger, anxiety, attraction – all vie for my first place emotion.

Worry etches furrows in a face that was smooth yesterday. He places his hands on my shoulders and kisses my forehead. "It's not what you think, Beau."

The door leading to the tarmac silhouettes his tall frame. At the steps to the plane, he turns and waves good-bye.

Only then, do I realize he calls me beautiful.

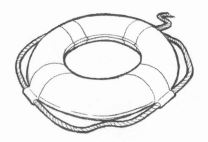

Nine

My mother strides toward a bank of pay phones lining the wall of the airport terminal. She picks up and dials a number from memory. Who is she calling?

"Hi! . . . Des Moines . . . Yes . . . Okay . . . Okay . . . Sure . . . Thanks."

"Mom, who was that?"

"Your grandmother. Let's go."

I have the same feeling I get when my hair is first braided, tight. Tight to the point of pain.

She strides out of the airport. My mother who meanders, wanders, halts, but never strides.

I follow, wondering if Troy is in the plane zooming overhead. "Where are we going?"

As usual, she doesn't answer. We just get in the car and go.

My mom stops at a bank that looks like an old black-and-white movie set: stone columns and a huge waiting area. Walking toward the teller, my mom's swirling skirt and tie-dye t-shirt may be *de rigueur* in Eugene, but in Des Moines they look deranged.

She asks for the manager and harasses him until he checks for a bank draft in her name. When he hands her the money, his attitude changes from snooty to obsequious. (Another Amber word. She says it's better than brown-nosing, which is disgusting.)

Instead of finding a health food store, we walk three blocks to an electronics store. Excitement bubbles through me like my first sip of soda. My voice rises to an almost squeal, "We're getting a smartphone!"

Pushing the door open with her shoulder, my mom says, "Your grandmother's orders."

Communication Central. Yeah, Grandma! Shifting my weight from one foot to the other, I scrutinize the accessory display.

My mother is such a technophobe, I'm certain I'll be carrying the new phone. And I won't be stuck listening to her hippy music on the radio!

Ordering the phone takes forever because my mother doesn't have a credit card. Something about private profit and social loss. We call my grandmother back, and thankfully, she knows how to buy a phone, over the phone.

When we get in the car, the first call I make is to Miles. TatCon. He doesn't pick up. I leave a message for Amber in case she checks them. I consider calling my dad, but why bother?

My mom stares at me, but I can't read her expression. Tired? Anxious? Guilty? Sober.

"I didn't sleep with Troy," she says.

I feel the burn rise. If my skin was pale like my mom's, I'd be bright red. "I don't care." But I do.

"I know what you're thinking. He was sad, honey. His mom left a few years ago. He doesn't know where she is."

White spots blur my vision and I explode. "You were in your underwear!"

My mother laughs. Laughs! "I did the laundry."

I do not want to think about this. My anger is a blanket, warm and safe. Safer than trusting her.

We are back on the highway. I can't do anything involving paper while we're moving, not without the possibility of puking. But pixels are a different matter.

I spend some time on an app for rating tattoos. Some of the work is so bad, I can't believe somebody would post it. My favorite is a badger: cute, fuzzy, and fierce.

Three protein bar wrappers lay at my feet and my water bottle is empty when I realize we have driven across Iowa. All I have is a hazy memory of cornfields and pig farms.

We drive to Davenport and stop for gas. The great expanse of the Mississippi flows slate-blue before us. "Mom, let's pull off at the next exit. We can dip our toes in the river." It may not be whatever that river is that runs through Paris, but it isn't the Willamette in Eugene.

She is mumbling, "With an 'm' and an 'i' and an 's, s, i' and an ippi and a pippi and a Mississippi."

"Hello, Mom!"

She swerves onto the exit ramp, definitely on autopilot.

Almost hitting her in the chin, I point. "Route 22, take a left." After directing her to a parking lot, I say, "Did you know the Mississippi runs through ten states? And it comes from an Ojibwa word that means 'Great River'?" I am loving the smartphone.

No answer. Worry glides through me gritty as river water. She hasn't said much since her contact with grandmother and our talk about laundry. Thinking about my mother and Troy still pisses me off.

Hard-as-stone tension lodges in my stomach. We're only a few hours away from Chicago. A few hours away from Oyster. When will we see him? Today? Tomorrow? I breathe in quick gasps. Maybe oxygen is an antidote for rotten shellfish.

At least my mother hasn't asked for the phone. Once he has our number, he can reach us anytime. I thrust those thoughts into the black hole of things not to think.

My mom finds a parking spot by a tree. She kicks off her sandals, abandons them by the front tire, and heads for the riverbank.

I place the cell phone and guidebook into the glove box. She's left the keys dangling in the ignition. I slip them out, lock the doors, and hide them in my shoe. Not very original, but I don't want to risk getting the door opener wet. I stick my shoes under the car, between the back tires, as far as I can reach.

When I roll up my jeans, sunshine pokes through the wispy high clouds and warms my legs. I step into the river. The bluish-green water swirls cool around my knees and my cuffs soak up the Mississippi.

I breathe in to the count of four, hold for three, breathe out for three. Repeat. By the third breath, my body relaxes. Anxiety and anger drift away on the current.

My mom hovers at the waterline. "If this was the Ganges,

86

we'd bathe our way to enlightenment."

I squish my toes into the mud. "John baptized Jesus in a river."

"Remind me again why I sent you to bible preschool?"

"It's all education, Mom!"

There is a shift. One second things are tense and tight, the next I feel happy and loose. It's normal between my mom and me again. I take a deep breath and close my eyes.

Opening them as I exhale the glinting sunlight beckons. I take another step. My bare toes catch on something buried on the bottom. Arms flap wide to save me from falling, but this is not solid ground. Sprawling face first into the muddy water I scramble to stand, but my legs are being swept downstream. I can't get them under me.

Panic fills my mouth, my nostrils, my lungs. Choking and coughing, I whirl around.

The current sucks me farther from shore, where the water flows the fastest. It is too deep to stand. The river pulls at my clothes. My legs, wrapped in soaking denim, drag me down. I try to kick, but it feels like they're made of anchors.

My meager attempt to swim becomes a battle. The Mississippi is winning.

I fight harder: the terror, the thundering river, the tremendous distance to the shore. It is too far – I cannot make it.

A wave washes over my head. Gasping and spluttering, I see a large tree trunk rushing toward me. I spin away from it, just missing its tangled roots.

The shore is nearer than I thought. Iowa is a lot closer than Illinois.

My mom is flapping her arms and screaming. She is too far away to reach me.

Alone. I struggle to survive: the river, the floating debris, the fear.

Exhaustion weighs me down, heavy as my waterlogged clothes. A shadow looms over me – the I-280 bridge. I strike out, hoping to grasp one of the cement supports. Kicking, contacting, and colliding. I whoosh by.

I hear people yell from a dock, "You can do it!" and "Get the next one!" I might die, but at least I have my own cheerleading squad.

I force myself to reach for the next column and cling to the wet cement, my grasp slipping, water flowing around me.

Someone calls, "Grab this!"

A rope dangles in the water. A man in a small motorboat angles away from the dock on the downriver side. "Put it around your waist!"

The rope is thick and stiff and stinks. Scrambling to hold it and the pillar, I realize that managing both is impossible. My brain screams, let go! But my fingers cling tighter. The rope slips through my grasp and I lose my grip on the stone.

The river is rushing me away from the bridge, away from people helping, away from my mother. The man reels in the line, ties on an orange lifesaver, moves the boat closer and throws it toward me again.

It hits my head. I am under. Water clogs my mouth, nose, ears.

I am too tired to keep struggling. It is so much easier to give up. Arms and legs heavy. Letting go, letting the water take me.

I feel Troy's kiss on my forehead. "Beau."

One thrust upward toward Troy and his kiss. Breaking the surface, my vision is orange. The life preserver! I pull myself through the hole. Bobbing far easier than a battle with the Mississippi.

My hands hold the rope hard. The man hauls me toward the boat, grabs my shirt at the shoulders. I tense, expecting the fabric to tear, the river to refuse to let me go.

But the material holds and he hefts me on board. Collapsed on the deck, a fishing reel pokes my butt cheek. I gag and sputter, hoping I won't puke the Mississippi into his boat.

He scratches the blond stubble on his chin and chuckles. I hadn't realized angels might need to shave. "Not the best place for a swim, young lady!"

I want to say something clever, but I am all out of snark. "Tripped." Ragged words press through my chattering teeth. "Current carried me." I untangle myself from the nylon line. "Thank you."

"Anytime. Just don't let it happen again!"

He laughs at his joke, but I am not in the mood to join him. My clothes are muddy and wet and I smell like fish. Old, left-out-in-the-sun-fish.

We stop at the dock and Star is waiting. Waiting for me, her difficult daughter.

I force myself to clamber out of the boat. My mother clings to me, soaking herself. At first I don't mind the hug, but ten seconds is long enough. "Mom, you're smothering me."

The man, his anchor tattoo blurred beneath the tawny hair on his forearm, pilots his boat away from the pier. "Tourists welcome in the great state of Iowa. But remember, the Mississippi's not made for swimming."

"Thank you!" I shout at his retreating back, but my throat is raw and a croak comes out.

The people who had gathered on the dock drift away. "God bless!" "Good luck!" Their daily ration of excitement doled out.

Drip, drop, plop. We stand alone and I am wondering why we are waiting. My energy puddles at my feet with the river water.

Star's eyes flash lightning anger. "What were you thinking?" A tornado of rage rips through her heading in my direction. "You shouldn't have gone so far out! Did you think you could swim to Illinois?" Her gale force voice shrieks, "You could have died!"

Head in hands, pummeled by her words, I endure. There is no response I can offer that will send the emotion spinning in a new direction. I know from experience, eventually the storm will pass. Anger, my mother's way to show she loves me. It doesn't last long.

Spent, we wander toward the car.

I am shivering, the June sun too weak to warm me. My clothes hang: wet and heavy, cold and irritating. Water drips from my jeans, leaving a trail of pockmarks in the dirt. My teeth chatter until my jaw hurts. Clenching doesn't help.

When we reach the car, I realize my mom is shivering, too. "Mom, are you okay?"

She doesn't answer, running her hand along the back of the Subaru over and over as if she can't recall how to spring the latch.

There is nowhere private to change. Mud splatters cover us

from shoulder to shin, as if we'd spent the morning wrestling pigs in a pen – and lost.

Thankfully, no one else is parked nearby. In the back seat, I wriggle out of my wet jeans, surprised there are no fish flopping in the faded denim. The dry clothes tug at my wet skin.

I step out. A few quick flips of my braids whip small chunks of mud through the air.

"Hey!" My mom has newly acquired freckles sprinkled around her smile.

"It's a good look for you, Mom. How about a new nickname? Mudmeasles or Dalmation?"

"Mudmeasle and the Dalmations. Maybe your dad's on tour with them." Her laughter blows away the last of her anger.

Relief trickles through me loosening the tension in my shoulders.

"My turn," she says and changes quickly.

We're back in the car. I navigate us to the highway and over the bridge. One glance at the churning water and even shutting my eyes doesn't protect me from the feeling of it closing over my head. Focusing on the horizon helps, but curling into a ball inside Miles's sweatshirt is better. I slump in the seat, my energy level on empty.

Star exits the highway just across the river in Milan, Illinois. She drives past the gas station into a small parking lot with a liquor store and a fast food restaurant with a giant "M" straddling the roof.

My muscles are limp with exhaustion. Only my brain still works, assessing our situation. My mother is mega-stressed, loaded with cash, low on drugs. Her top priority? Buzz in a bottle.

Unable to open my door farther than a few inches, because she parked so close to the car next to us, I scramble over the driver's seat to get out. The sweatshirt hood hangs over my face, but I keep my mom's feet in sight.

Maybe I should have stayed in the car. Maybe kids aren't allowed in liquor stores in Illinois. Maybe this time the police will stop her.

When she opens the door the stench of greasy fast food hits me like a slap, seizing my stomach. This is not a liquor store.

My organic-only mother, who threw out blueberries I bought with my own money because they weren't OG. Diner food is one thing, but fast food? Has she had a brain transplant?

My mom smiles at my scowl. "You didn't know I like this stuff, did you?"

At the moment, she could eat a deep-fried Twinkie for all I care. The girl behind the counter, whose heavy eye makeup clashes with her company shirt, is giving my mom's new freckles funny looks.

I shuffle my way to a hard atomic tangerine chair.

A few minutes later my mom arrives with a burger big enough to feed a family of four and a colossal mound of fries.

Potatoes, oil – things I can eat.

The taste is nothing like the homemade fries Amber's dads make. But I am ravenous. The pile has almost disappeared when I realize my lips are beginning to tingle.

Potatoes, oil – it can't be the fries.

The air contains molecules of beef and chicken. Combined with the shock from almost drowning could be enough to trigger a reaction. My throat feels thick, scratchy. Maybe it's just the Mississippi I swallowed.

My mother, the oblivious one, is munching away. Should I tell her my cheeks and the tip of my nose are numb?

No.

I close my eyes to focus on my body. My breathing is shallow and it feels like there is a tight band constricting across my chest. Time for the first line in my defense against an allergic reaction. I open a gold packet, plop two tablets into a cup of water, and down the fizzy mixture.

My mom asks, "Are you okay?"

I want to nod my head, but it comes out a shake instead.

"Oh, no. The fries!" She leaps out of her chair and dashes over to the counter.

It's getting hard to think. There is something I need, but I can't remember what it is.

My mom rushes back carrying a piece of cardboard. "It's the fries." She reads the ingredients, "Who the hell puts gluten, dairy, and beef in a French fry?"

I have no answer and one question. Am I going anaphylactic?

She hustles me out of the building and into the car. "You'll be fine. You'll be fine." Is she trying to convince me, herself, or the universe?

I fumble the antihistamines, taking forever to get them out of that stupid packaging. Swallow. Cool water soothes my tight throat. Should I use the epipen?

The nine-one-one-ambulance-emergency-room route is not my first choice. They treat you like you are an idiot who doesn't know to stay away from allergens. They ask zillions and zillions of questions. They stick needles in you. Eight hours of prying, poking, prodding. No thanks.

Memory: I am nine. Rice at a potluck is made with chicken broth, but I don't know that until I can hardly breathe. I go into the bathroom and follow the directions on the injector. The hypodermic is knitting-needle-thick and hurts so bad I can't breathe at all. Then, in a rush, my lungs begin to work. Later, I learn that you can go back into a reaction after your twenty minute grace period from the epinephrine.

Sometimes the antihistamines are enough. My head rests against the seat, eyes closed, I monitor my breathing. My mom pats my hand over and over and over. Maybe it's comforting her, but it's annoying me and I wish she would just drive, even if we only go thirty miles an hour.

I almost died twice today. The clock blinks 12:42. Actually, twice in one hour. My new record.

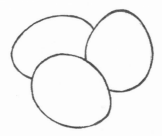

Ten

The Subaru slugs along at forty-five miles an hour, smelling like old grease and dead cow. The closer we get to Chicago, the harder it is to suck in air.

I focus on the tension in my chest, my stomach, my thighs, willing the muscle groups to relax. Failing.

I do my in four, hold three, out three breathing. It's not the Mississippi calamity, not the clown food.

The sky starts spitting rain. My mom turns on the windshield wipers. They whoosh back and forth: Oy...ster, Oy...ster.

I turn on the radio hoping they listen to Jerry Garcia in Illinois, hoping it won't remind her that our current destination is Chicago.

The classic oldies station plays Jimi and Janis and Jim. She sings along to "All Along the Watchtower" and "Piece of My Heart," and "Riders on the Storm."

I open the window and keep my mouth shut, the moist, cool breeze flying in my face. The sign looms ahead, "Welcome to Indiana! Land of the Hoosiers." I have no idea what a Hoosier is, but I am ready to celebrate. Air swooshes in and out of my lungs, easy-peasy.

My mom left Oyster rotting!

We stop for gas in Gary. The phone is coming in handy, a lifeline to all the health food stores across the country. Amazing, people in the heartland of America are eating organic. "Mom, there's a place we can buy food a few miles from here."

She puts the nozzle back on the pump. "We don't need to buy any food. We're going to Valparaiso."

Another pot stop. My voice squeaks as I feign innocence, "Why?"

My mom's lips, cheeks, eyes exude happiness. "We're visiting my friend, Mary."

"Does she know we're coming?"

"Yes. I called her before we left Eugene."

"Does she know about my allergies?"

My mom slams the car door. "It'll be okay."

What will be okay? There won't be anything to eat or the hospital is nearby?

Another hour in the car and my butt is numb. I navigate the country roads, certain we are lost. "Mom, can you pull over and we'll ask for directions?"

"No need to." Past a field of something green, she makes a right into a driveway. Her voice rises to a shout, "We're here."

The faded yellow home has blue hydrangeas lining either side of the front door. A girl who looks about eleven dashes up the steps to the back porch. The screen door swings closed behind her, almost catching her long, brown braids.

My mom parks the car between the house and the barn. A woman approaches: Star's height, except thin and wiry with wrinkles lining her mouth and eyes. Wiping her hands on a kitchen towel, she stuffs it into the back pocket of her jeans. Her arms open wide and my mother runs into them.

Star's shoulders shake and tears flow down her face.

Mary pats her on the back. "It's been too long, sis."

Sister? I close my mouth before a fly buzzes its way in, though breathing through my nose makes the farm smells more obvious. Even the dirt has that after-the-rain-odor.

A teenager steps out of the shadows of the barn wearing overalls without a shirt. "Hi." His muscles are dirty and hard.

Mary steps out of the hug. "This is my son, Neal."

His face brightens with one of those make-you-feel-like-grinning smiles. "Are we cousins?"

She brushes some dirt from his hair. "No, not really. Star and I are just real good friends."

A tiny flame of hope for a real family snuffed out.

Neal shuffles his feet, dirt rising around his construction boots. "What's your name?"

"Rainbeau."

He stops his two-step. "Really?"

Normal in Eugene is odd in Indiana.

Mary throws him an over-the-shoulder-don't-be-impolite look and leads us toward the back porch. "Time for lemonade."

I have to ask. "Is it made with honey?"

Mary focuses on me, one brow lifted.

I gaze at the ground, shoulders slumped, hating that I have to explain. "I'm allergic to bees and honey."

Mary runs her hand softly across my braids. "No problem. It's just plain old white sugar, lemons, and water."

Her eyes are a pretty combination of light brown with gold and dark specks. In my mind, I see the pencils I will need to sketch them.

Mary and Star relax on the faded green striped pillows of an old porch swing, Neal heads through the screen door and I choose a chair that rocks and creaks. A cool breeze dries the kitchen towels hanging on a line strung between the pillars. A small boy peers at us from the corner of the house.

Star whispers to Mary. I catch one word, "pot," and my heart feels as wrung out as a rind of lemon.

Mary says, "Not here."

"The barn?" Star asks.

Mary's eyes open wide and I can almost see her thoughts reflected there: flames licking the walls of the barn. "There's no place for that on a farm."

My mother's face crumples.

Thank you, Mary.

I play peek-a-boo with the boy as he creeps toward the steps. He halts when Star asks, "How many children do you have?"

Mary smiles. "Five."

My mother slips off her Birkenstocks and tucks up her legs. "Do they all have Down?"

What a question!

But Mary doesn't look offended.

"Yes. Fifteen years ago my folks kicked me out pregnant and

unmarried. So I came to work here. Peter was an old widower who wanted someone to do his cooking and cleaning. He loved Neal – taught him all kinds of things."

Neal pushes the door open with his shoulder, carefully balancing a tray with a pitcher of lemonade and some glasses. "I can fix the tractor."

Mary's smile fills with pride. "After that, folks and social services figured I could handle more. With God's help, I have."

A baby cries and Mary calls out, "Faith, honey, bring Angel here, please."

Faith, the girl with the braids, joins us on the porch with a baby in her arms. She sways and hums until the little one settles.

The little boy jumps into Mary's lap. "This is Gary."

He makes a face at me so I stick out my tongue and roll my eyes.

Mary says, "Looks like you've found a friend," and sets him down.

He lifts a box from a shelf and points to me.

Mary sips her lemonade. "Be careful he's a checker shark!"

We settle in for a game with Neal nearby, watching.

My mom asks the question I've been wondering, "Five?"

Mary sighs and smoothes the wrinkles by her eyes. "Emily arrived when she was six, but her health was real bad. We couldn't save her." She nods toward a huge oak. "She's buried next to Peter. It near broke his heart when she died and he didn't last the year."

My mom holds her friend's hand. "I'm so sorry."

Mary smiles small and tight.

Faith places the baby in Mary's arms. "I love you," Mary tells her daughter. Faith leans down and rubs her cheek against her mom's.

She kisses her mom and plops down by Neal, leaning against him. He puts his arm around her. "Gary's going to win," she says.

She's probably right.

A comfortable silence settles, patient and peaceful. Time passes languid as a lazy lizard stretched out in the sun.

I look from the board to the baby who stares with heavy lidded eyes, kicking her legs. Mary pulls up the little shirt and blows a raspberry on her tummy. Her chubby arms flail and her giggle makes everyone smile.

Gary shouts, "Crown me!" and jumps my king.

Three turns later, I wait as he struggles to place a piece on top of mine.

He announces, "You only have one king. I have three." After seven more moves, Gary gives me a consolation hug and a slobbery victory kiss. "I won!"

Mary stands up with the baby in her arms, "Peter used to tell me that God gives everyone a calling. Maybe checkers is Gary's." She kisses Angel. "This is mine."

Sadness seeps through me and takes up residence in my chest. A real family: loving people, living together, caring for one another.

Mom are you paying attention? Serial manfriends are not family.

Mary hands Faith the baby. I pat the soft downy hair on Angel's head. Ignoring Faith's frown, I ask, "Can I hold her?"

She hugs the baby tighter and shakes her head.

100

Nibbling on my thumb, I wonder if I'd be so possessive if I had a sister.

Mary gathers the empty glasses and asks, "Why don't you help me?"

Neal hands me his and I stack it with the others.

"Stay for dinner?" Gary asks.

"Of course." Mary insists. "Ham and peas with homemade biscuits. Rainbeau are you allergic to any other foods?"

I follow her into the kitchen. "Ham and peas sound good, but I can't have gluten."

"Ice cream?"

"No. Or dairy."

She hands me a bowl of peas that need shelling. "That must be difficult."

I shrug and search the floor for a dropped pea. "I'm used to it."

She lifts my chin with her finger and I am staring into her complex, beautiful eyes. "I understand hard. Life can be hard. But that deepens our challenge to search for God's grace."

A glimmer of understanding passes through me. "Grace?"

"Look around you. Unexpected help when you need it, the feeling of oneness with all God's creation, a child's smile."

I want to believe her, but something stops me. Pessimism? Proof? If God is out there, then why do bad things happen? I don't want to confront Mary with my questions. I'm not sure I'm ready for the answers.

Faith hands me napkins and we set the table. Neal rolls Angel's crib into the dining room. When everyone is seated, we hold hands and take turns sharing something that makes us thankful. Mary and Neal say, "New friends." Star follows their lead.

Faith says, "Angel."

My heart pumps faster bringing heat to my face. I don't know if I should say what I'm feeling.

Gary leans toward me and in a very loud whisper says, "Go ahead."

"I'm thankful to be with a family," I say softly to the folds of tablecloth in my lap. When I look up, my mom is sitting stiffly in her chair, but Mary and the kids are nodding.

It's Gary's turn for gratitude. He shouts, "I'm thankful for butter!"

Everyone laughs as they pass the food. It reminds me of Amber's house when her cousins are visiting. I miss Amber and Miles, even though it's been less than a week since I saw them. They may not be my real family, but they're the closest thing I have.

Everyone is talking at the same time. Neal silences his siblings with a look. He seems so much older than I am, even though he's only fifteen.

After we clear the table and wash and dry the dishes, Gary pulls me by the hand to show me the hen house. The last thing I want to do is stick my hand under a chicken and pull out an egg. But he insists. My effort is rewarded with a peck from the disturbed mother and a giggle from Gary. Much quicker, he shows me an egg he's managed to get without rustling the hen's feathers. "It will be a chick."

I may be a city girl, but I do know that much.

"Or breakfast," he says, putting it back.

The pigpen is next on Gary's agenda. Lucky me. Piglets squeal in a game of porcine tag. Giant hogs, the size of ponies, have finished their dinner and are rooting around for more. The fence standing between us is small protection if they decide I'm dessert.

As we head to the barn, we hear a cow low. While Neal milks the mama, Faith holds the calf and explains, "She's upset. We usually do this before dinner."

Neal wants to teach me how to pull on the teats, but I am not touching a cow's private parts.

He fills the bucket. Hiss, hiss, plink, hiss, hiss, plink.

A mama cat climbs the ladder to the hayloft, a mouse swinging from her jaws.

Gary points to her. "Kittens!"

I don't see any pointy ears in the straw.

A wet stream hits my cheek. I swipe the milk away and bite back the "Eeww!" that is ready to leap from my mouth.

Neal is hard at work milking, but Faith's shoulders shake with suppressed laughter.

I am thankful the warm milk didn't go near my mouth. I've had enough of allergies and animals to last a lifetime or two or three.

After chores, we play hide and seek. I haven't played since I was ten. Faith makes it safely to base shouting, "Olly, olly, oxenfree!" I've forgotten the rules.

It is dusk when Mary stands on the back porch calling for us. Her faded clothes lit from within. My mother stands nearby, hesitantly grasping a column, bright purple paisley a poor attempt at camouflaging emptiness.

Mary hugs her children and me, too. "Neal, you share with Gary tonight. Go inside and set things up. We have company."

My mom says, "Really, we should be going."

Mary pats her arm. "Of course you'll stay."

I want to leap for joy. Stay! I might even learn to enjoy milking a cow and plucking eggs from underneath cantankerous hens. "Mom, please!"

"For the night, if it's not too much trouble."

Of course, she only meant for the night. Disappointment caps an overfull day. Until now, I've ignored the exhaustion weighing on my bones heavy as waterlogged clothes.

Mary says, "Go on in and tell Neal and Faith you can watch a movie together after the little ones are settled." She and Star sit on the porch swing, two women in their thirties looking like children as they rock in rhythm and laugh, loud and long.

Later, I cuddle under the quilt of a real bed. We've only been here a few hours and already this peaceful place feels like home. Cicadas and crickets and peepers lull me to sleep.

In the morning, warmth and light filter through the lace curtains. Someone shouts, "Let's get Rainbeau!" and the room fills with laughter. Faith extends one finger to touch the beads in my hair. Gary jumps on the bed and my braids bounce out of reach.

Neal stands solid in the doorway, Angel in his arms. "Breakfast is ready." They dash madder than hatters out of the room.

My clean clothes are neatly folded on top of the dresser. I pull on shorts and a faded red t-shirt with a tribal design, thinking of Miles and the shop. This is the only place we've been where I don't miss him so much. I head downstairs humming "What a Wonderful World."

On the table, there are huge platters of steaming blueberry pancakes. Amethyst hydrangeas bloom in a white pitcher.

Everyone is seated, waiting for me. "Sorry."

Grace at breakfast is a quick, "Thank you, Lord, for the gifts you bestow on us today. Please make us worthy to receive them."

The family has been up for hours doing their chores. I tell Neal, "You could have woken me. I would have helped."

Mary passes the plate of pancakes. "The two of you needed to sleep. Your mom told me about your swim yesterday."

Gary begs, "Tell us the story!"

I stare at the bacon on my plate. No pancakes for me. "It was stupid."

Gary sticks his head below table level, looking up at me. "I do stupid, too. Sometimes."

If we weren't at the table, I'd hug him. I relive my near-drowning-in-the-Mississippi. With a real family surrounding me, it doesn't seem so frightening.

Star adds her point of view, as if she was the center of the story. Why does everything always have to be about her?

Gary jumps up from his seat and pretends to swim to the kitchen for more butter, making us all laugh. Five-years-old and he understands that he makes us happy.

Why is it when I do or say something and people laugh, it seems like they're making fun of me?

After breakfast, everyone helps clean up. I wash each dish slowly, carefully, trying to postpone the inevitable. When the last plate had been dried and placed in the cupboard, Star says, "Time to go. Your grandmother's expecting us."

A ladybug crawls along the window ledge. I would trade places with it, if only I could stay.

My mom is rummaging in the back seat of the Subaru. She places the Buddha on the roof and opens her suitcase to put away her toothbrush and her clothes. For her, leaving is business as usual.

I throw my backpack in the car. After seven days on the road, I've finally found a place where I'm comfortable. And now it's time to move on.

Maybe I shouldn't care. But I do.

My mom gets lots of practice with good-byes from her revolving manfriends.

It takes a while for all the hugs to go around. Each one fills me with a little bit of love, a little bit of sadness.

Neal is telling me their address and phone number as I punch it into the phone. I look up to see Mary in my mom's turquoise paisley shirt, my mom in Mary's clothes – brown and tan and blue.

Neal writes down our cell number. He gives me a quick hug, his muscles firm against my chest.

We get in the car and wave out the window. Backing down the driveway, we are leaving family, not traveling toward it.

Eleven

Welcome to the state of boredom. A state the size of a Subaru. A state where there is nothing to do.

I've had enough of the smartphone and its time-waster apps and facts. I'd like to actually get a call. Or a text. "Next stop?" I ask my mom.

She looks totally different in Mary's clothes – like she's morphed into a conservative talk-show host. "Bala Cynwyd."

Fantasyland, here we come! "No, really, where are we going?"

"Really, Bala Cynwyd."

"And this strange place is where?

"Near Philadelphia."

We've gone over the river and through the woods. Actually I've gone in the river, through the woods, across the plains, and over the mountains and we're still not close to grandmother's house.

"Why are we stopping there?"

"An old friend of mine. I think you'll like him."

Who knew my mom had so many old friends?

She spells "Valparaiso" and "Bala Cynwyd" for me so I can check the route on the phone. "We still have to go through most of Indiana, Ohio, and Pennsylvania."

"We'll stop for the night somewhere." My mom's "somewhere" could be anywhere.

Since being with Mary, my mom hasn't mentioned marijuana. Come to think of it, since Troy left my mom's been driving hundreds of miles a day and hasn't gotten high once. I could get used to this new mom.

My feet twitch and jiggle a short version of a happy dance, but I can't seem to shake the itch and niggle of doubt.

Mary filled up the cooler, so we only stop once for a gas-and-bathroom break. The rest of the time we are stuck in a box hurtling along at forty-eight miles an hour.

With Indiana and part of Ohio behind us, we stop in a small town, past Akron, north of Cleveland. My mom has driven for almost seven hours – her new record.

"Time for a break," she says and pulls into a cheap hotel. No pool, no cable.

The room is an older version of where we stayed with Troy. "Can't we stay somewhere nice?"

"No need to waste money." She unlocks the door and turns on the light. "We're only here to sleep."

The cell phone rings and I recognize Oyster's number. My stomach takes up residence in my throat along with those other organs I'd know if I was better in biology.

Then just as quickly my insides plummet as I realize he is in Chicago, which is a whole lot closer than Eugene. I could tell my mom it's a wrong number.

Except she reaches for the ringing phone. My fingers tremble as I hand it to her.

Her face changes from happy seashell pink surprise to embarrassed salmon as she answers the call. "I'm sorry. . . things happened . . . I forgot." Her cheeks are splotchy sangria highlighted with tears.

I hear him yell, "I'll kill you!" Slam!

The line is done doggy dead.

I flop down on the hard-as-the-floor bed. She'd forgotten to meet him. I didn't remind her. "Is he coming here?"

My mom wipes the back of her hand across her cheek. "No."

"How did he get our number?"

She rubs her finger along the stickers on her suitcase. "Last night I left a message explaining what happened. First Bob and Troy and then you in the river and a reaction." Her cheeks are blotched, but the tears are gone. "I'll go get the other bags."

She thinks her pot is in the other bag, but I saw her put it in her suitcase. When the goin' gets tough, my mom gets high.

Once again, I'll have to worry about the police coming, about them taking her away or taking me away. There is only one way to wipe out the worry.

I ransack her suitcase. The car door slams. My fingers grasp the slippery plastic bag and I run the three steps to the bathroom, locking the door. At flush number five, some of it is still floating.

Star knocks. "Where's my baggie?"

Flush, flush, flush. Flush number eight and even the papers are gone.

She is pounding on the door, yelling, "What did you do?"

"Stop making so much noise!" I hiss. "It's gone."

"No!"

There is a banging on the wall and an irate voice shouts, "Shut up in there!"

"Mom, someone's going to call the police."

She sobs, "You don't understand. What if I threw away your epipens? How would you feel?"

I soar from self-righteous to self-preservation in six seconds. My epipens? Without them I could die. I whip open the bathroom door, rage roaring through me. "It is not the same!"

My mother sits on the bed, shoulders curled inward. "I need the pot, just like you need your allergy meds."

I fight the urge to throttle her, grabbing her shoulders instead of her throat. "Marijuana is a drug, not a medication." Power courses through me as I shake her, her head whipping back and forth. I spit out the words, "You are a drug addict."

Disgusted, I drop my hands. She pushes herself to standing. I see her arm move backward, as if in slow motion, her hand rises coming toward me. Nearer and nearer until I feel the sting of the slap across my face. She shouts, "How dare you!"

My mother has never hit me. Not as a toddler when I tore up her rolling papers, not as a ten-year-old when I broke her bong, not last year when I forgot to give her the message her supplier was going out of town.

The tears build up like rain inside me. Damn! I will not let them flood. My whole body aches for a hug, for my mother to tell me I'm more important than her drugs.

She grabs the car keys and flings herself into the pouring rain. Not even one small glance my way. She has the cash to replace her stash. But how much opportunity could there be in this small town in rural Ohio? Maybe she just needs some time to calm down.

A girl can hope.

I throw my backpack on the lime and olive drab bedspread. Red-striped curtains and fuzzy yellow wallpaper – Hell probably has better décor.

Adrenaline drains from my system turning into who-knows-what chemical. I am a discarded soda can on the edge of the highway. But the slight bit of fizz that's left pings through me and I do not want to go to bed.

I'm all alone in a scuzzy motel. Unfortunately, the cooler did not make it into the room before my mother rushed off. But I have water and chocolate, *The Blue Girl* in my backpack and the cell phone. It could be worse.

I close the curtains, making sure they overlap, and latch the chain on the door. Then I notice a hole the size of a nickel on the wall across from the bed. What's weird is that it's dark, then light, then dark again. When I stand up to take a better look the pattern reoccurs, but not in a regular tempo.

It's an eye!

Someone in the next room is watching me. I jump toward the bathroom to get out of the line of sight.

A huge, ancient television sits on the dresser. I shove my shoulder against it, trying to barricade the opening. It moves a few inches. The cord is too short. Unplugged, one more mighty push, and the hole is blocked.

Miniscule spider feet break dance on my skin. I search for more holes, on the walls, and the ceiling, and the bathroom. There couldn't be one in the floor, could there?

Webs of paranoia cling to me. I fling my arms out as if I could brush them away and wonder if the Peeping Tom is watching. I suppose that's sexist, but I've never heard of a Peeping Tomasina.

I check the room three more times for peepholes before I decide to call the front desk. When I pick up the phone, it's dead. I push all the buttons, shake the receiver, check the plug and the wires. Nothing.

Useless. I have the cell phone, so I can't call my mom. It's the last night of TatCon so Miles is busy. Grandmother? I've never met her and she's dying. I don't want her to worry about me. I want her to love me.

Am I safer staying in the room or going to talk to the person at the front desk? If I stay, the creep might be waiting for me to go to sleep. My mind latches onto scenes from the one horror movie I've watched in my whole life. If I leave, the pervert might grab me. If I call the police they'll take me away when my mom shows up with her drugs.

"Improvise, adapt, and overcome," I tell myself and throw on my sneakers, hoping Amber's decorations won't get ruined in the rain. I grab my pack and the room key, close the door as quietly as I can and look around for anything suspicious. The parking lot is empty. I race-walk to the front desk, hopping over puddles.

"Excuse me," I say to an older woman with glasses hanging around her neck. "The phone isn't working."

"Oh, my no. The phones haven't worked for over a month."

"Oh." What I thought was a star earring is really a tattoo. The woman has to be eighty. I imagine her a circus performer, covered in gray-green, faded, drooping tats.

Nasty.

A charcoal colored cat jumps onto the counter and rubs its back against her wrist. "Is anything wrong, dear?"

For one second, I think she is talking to the cat. I step toward the door and hesitate. "No. Thank you."

I can't rely on an old woman and a cat.

When I get back to the room I consider a steamy shower, but in my mind all I hear is screeching violins.

The last motel was Beverly Hills chic compared to this. Was it really only two nights ago?

I dig through my backpack for my book and find a crumpled piece of paper. It's a note from Troy.

> *Dear Beau,*
>
> *I'm sorry that you got the wrong idea about your mom and me. Nothing happened. Honest. She was doing the laundry and it made me think of my mom. My mom left six years ago with no note, nothing. My dad never talks about it. I still cry sometimes. Your mom was real sweet. She held me. It wasn't more than that. I swear. I hope you believe me.*
>
> *Your friend,*
> *Troy*
> *020-928-2967*

I punch a rolled-up towel. Each hit for someone: Troy

for letting me think he'd slept with my mom, Troy's mom for leaving, Troy's dad for getting hurt, my dad for never being around when I need him. There are so many hits for my mom I lose count. I beat the towel until I am hollow, arms aching.

God, where are you?

I crawl into bed still in my clothes. I will stay awake.

The door is shaking, chain rattling, someone pounding. I know there is a serial killer on the other side. A scream sticks in my throat and I cannot force it out.

I wake up, furious that I've fallen asleep. The thumping begins again. I can breathe, but it seems to be my only working bodily function.

Finally, I force myself out of bed, phone in hand, fumbling with the buttons.

"Rainbeau."

How does he know my name? What do I tell the police?

"Rainbeau!"

Wait. It's a woman's voice. Peeping Tomasina?

"Rainbeau open the door!"

I scramble to unlock it and my mom stumbles in.

Her clothes are filthy and torn, her eyes wild. She collapses on the bed and curls into a fetal position.

Panic claws it's way through me, but I cannot crumble. I force myself to think. "Mom, should I call the police?"

The quivering lump of khaki that is my mother moves from side to side and I guess that is a no. I nudge her to sit, and then guide her toward the bathroom.

She has to change. The smell: overpowering body odor and

blood with a hint of fear. But no pot.

I go back to the room to grab leggings and a shirt. When I return, she is cowering, naked, bruised and battered.

Shattered shards of memory poke and cut me: a tongue in my ear, a hard-on. But there is no time for my feelings.

It is 4:08 am and there is a pervert next door. And my mom…my mom…

There is no time to shower. After she changes, I walk her toward the car and help her into the backseat. I throw our bags in the way back and slam the trunk door. She still stinks, but there is nothing I can do about that.

My hand grips the keys, leaving a mark on my palm. I climb behind the wheel, close my eyes and press my fingers against the lids. I will not drive.

When I look up, I see light reflecting off the mirror. It's coming from the room next door. Tiny shocks shoot from my shoulders to my wrists. We cannot stay here.

I turn around. Behind the curtain there is a shadow of a man. I have to drive.

How hard could it be? My mom's autogeek manfriend let me drive around a field. Once.

Jiggling the shift, it is as if the autogeek is sitting beside me, barking instructions.

I push the gas pedal and the car lurches forward. The indicator on the dash reads "D," not "R."

I switch gears and stomp down hard. The car jolts backward. A heavy object hits my seat with a thud. Oops, I'd forgotten to buckle my mom's seatbelt.

Too much pressure on the brakes and she flops onto the

back seat. Looking over my shoulder to check, we almost hit a parked car. I jerk the wheel and spin a one-eighty. My mom doesn't move.

Sucking the cool night air into my lungs, I hold it until they ache. And let it out in a whoosh, applying slow pressure to the gas pedal. Easing my way out of the parking lot, up the exit ramp, onto the highway.

I focus on two things: breathing and the line in the middle of the road.

Twelve

Inching down the highway in the dark. Too bad there isn't a go-painfully-slow-for-those-who-don't-know-how-to-drive lane.

Hours go by before the sun rises and only the crows are awake.

My mom is still sacked out in the back. I try to imagine what happened to her, but the fear builds up and I cannot force it into the black hole of forgetting.

A siren sounds and my death grip on the wheel is the only thing preventing me from driving into a cow pasture. How long have those lights been flashing?

"Piglets and little brown mice!" The Amber saying pops out of my mouth. I wish she was here. Or better yet, I was there.

The police will search my mom. They will find her drugs. They will arrest me.

The officer pulls his car next to the Subaru and points. Right.

I should be pulling over.

Do they have handcuffs that fit small fourteen-year-olds?

I guide the car onto the shoulder and shivers set my body shaking. Great! He'll think I'm the drug addict.

Do I get out of the car or stay in?

Holding my breath forces my feelings inside. The shakes subside. Before I can get the door open, the officer is right next to me.

He motions for me to roll down the window. When I do, he says, "Breathe."

I slide my gaze to the left, but all I see is a neatly tucked in shirt.

He squats down and rests his arms on the door, glancing at my mom. "Why don't you tell me what's going on?"

My brain knows I'm not supposed to incriminate myself. My mouth does not. I yammer away, as if on speed. I hadn't realized I was so desperate to share the horrors of the past twelve hours.

The police officer puts his hand up. "Whoa, let me get this straight: Your mom left you in a hotel by yourself and she came back hours later in pretty bad shape."

"And the Peeping Tom and the old lady with the tats and the cat."

His eyebrow rises, but he doesn't interrupt.

Pleading, on the verge of whining, I say, "I had to get us out of there."

"And your mom's been passed out all this time?"

My teeth press against my lip as I nod. Taking her to the hospital would be better than jail. There aren't any convenient bees to send me there with an allergic reaction.

Then he asks the question that I have been dreading my whole life. The question that school counselors and teachers and doctors never ask.

His voice is soft, maybe kind, "What drugs is she on?"

I hold my breath and begin to disappear, but not in the one-with-God way. In the erasing-Rainbeau's-existence way. His fingers gently squeeze my arm, preventing me from floating into the dark. "I don't know." I hear the words before I realize I've spoken.

He wakes up Star, talks to her, has her walk the line on the road. She seems fragile, but calm. She lets him search the car, cooler, and the bags.

"Mom! You don't have to do this!"

I do not want to go to jail. I fling myself out of the car, ready to confront the policeman.

He slams the back hatch and smiles at me. "All clean."

"Really?" I did not say that.

"Really. Your mom will be okay. She gave me the name of the hotel and I'll have the police there check it out."

And? I know what is next. I put my hands out, my chin touching my chest.

His boots are reflect-the-face-of-the-guilty shiny. "Rainbeau."

He knows my name and I can't help but look up, into his olive drab eyes. The trembling starts again. My teeth sink into the cuticle of my thumb ripping off a piece of skin.

"Just don't drive again until you're old enough."

He walks me to the passenger side and opens the door. "And if you're in trouble, call us, we're here to help."

I slide in, buckle-up, and find my voice. "Thank you. For not arresting us."

My mom takes her place behind the wheel and we drive down the highway, silent for a long time.

I don't need the iPod. The words of a song keep running through my head:

Luck, you found me at last
You'd forsaken me in the past
You're here with me now I beg you to stay
Please don't go, don't go away...

Whatever happened to my mom is my fault. If I hadn't flushed her pot, she wouldn't have left last night and she wouldn't have . . . "Are you hurt bad?"

My mom doesn't look at me. "I'll be okay, honey. Don't worry."

How can I not? "Will you tell me what happened?"

"No."

My nails rake across the flash I've drawn on my jeans. "Why not? Why do you always have to keep secrets?"

She shakes her head, looking at the road. "To protect you."

The pressure that began when we started this trip, that increased with Oyster and Bob and Troy, that intensified with the Peeping Tom and the policeman...

Explodes.

"PROTECT ME!" My voice projects loud enough to be heard in Winnemucca. "Is that what you call sleeping half-naked with a teenager and eating in places where I have a reaction and watching me fall into the Mississippi and abandoning me, and . . . and . . . Oyster!"

She shepherds the Subaru onto the shoulder.

Now I understand the phrase "blood boiling" because mine is fiery lava, bubbling, about to blow. All the times, because of her, I was alone and scared and in danger: left at her friend's house overnight when the dog bit me, abandoned in a tent the first time I got my period, the time she was too high to take me to the emergency room when I had an anaphylactic reaction.

"Protect me is what a real parent would do!"

She sits in the driver's seat with tears and snot flowing down her face. It's disgusting. I dig through my backpack and hand her a tissue.

She does not thank me. She does not argue. She does not apologize.

She pulls back onto the highway.

My heart cracks, pumping pent-up pain through my veins to the rhythm: not lovable, not lovable.

We drive and drive and drive until the rolling hills of Pennsylvania lull me to sleep.

I wake up as my mother parks the car near an old theatre. The marquee says "Bala."

Old buildings, rusty red brick and carved stone, line the street. "Where are we?"

"Bala Cynwyd."

"Ballyhoo?"

"Bala Cynwyd."

Right. "And who are we visiting this time?"

She gets out of the car, waits for me, and locks it. "His name is Jayce Raleigh. He used to work security at the concerts."

"Does he know we're coming?"

"I told his personal assistant."

The old buildings hover over us holding secrets. "What kind of security guard has a personal assistant?"

My mom waits for the traffic to pass before crossing the street. "The kind that owns a multinational executive protection agency."

I match my strides to hers. "How well do you know him?"

She looks at me and her eyes slide away. Are there any men my mother hasn't slept with?

That is something I definitely don't need to know.

I imagine Jayce a giant of a white guy pumped up like the Terminator in that old movie, crew cut, sunglasses. His multinational corporation owning a giant glass tower with a perfect view of the skyline.

In front of us is boring white stone, lacking the fancy architectural extras of the buildings on either side. "Are you sure this is it?"

Star checks the address. "1420. We're here."

We have to get buzzed in at the entrance, which is strange because this is the incognito of incognito, Suburbia, USA.

My mother walks over to the security desk in tights and an oversized t-shirt. It wouldn't take a fashionista to know these are her pajamas. I shuffle behind, embarrassed enough for both of us.

Under the tie-dye my mother's back hardens. "We're here to see Jayce Raleigh."

The security guard snickers. "He's busy."

"Tell him Elizabeth Swift is here."

Elizabeth? In fourteen years I have never heard anyone call

my mom anything but Star. Elizabeth? Maggots of betrayal erode my self-confidence. Do I even know my own mother? Is my own name really Rainbeau?

When she turns toward me, her shoulder and eyebrow rise.

Apology or admission?

The guard is on the phone. He nods a few times before hanging up and escorts us to the elevator. When he steps near my mom, his flared nostrils tell me she still smells of sweat, dirt, and fear.

The office version of a Ferrari awaits us, everything chrome and black. The receptionist's eyebrows disappear beneath her bangs and her Egyptian blue eyeglasses slide down her nose. Her voice quavers, caught between a statement and a question, "Yes?"

My mother strides to the desk, but her hands are twitching. "We're here to see Jayce."

All we can see of the woman behind the desk is disgust on her twenty-something face. "Let's take you to the conference room, shall we?"

She clicks down the hall, steady on her four inch heels, brown hair brushing her shoulders. Opening the third door on the left, she ushers us in. Black bookshelves and a matching conference table would make it feel like a tomb if the fourth wall wasn't a giant window facing the Philadelphia skyline. A faint odor of cigars lingers in the cool gray curtains and carpeting.

I circle the room and ask, "Now what?"

My mother is already seated. "We wait."

I drop my backpack into a chair and unzip it, reaching for pad and pencils. Taking notes on décor for when I have my own tattoo shop. Perched on the bookshelf is an eagle holding the scales of justice. I just finish sketching a flash version of it when the door opens.

A deep I'm-always-in-charge voice says, "Hello, ladies." Jayce Raleigh fills the room with energy pulsing off his dark brown six-foot-something body. "Lizzy." His face softens for a moment. "What can I do for you?"

The steel in my mom's back has been replaced with aluminum foil. "This is my daughter, Rainbeau."

He nods his head at me. I have been dismissed, his focus is on my mother.

Twiddling the Om symbol hanging around her neck, she asks, "Can we talk?" and shifts her head at me. Her nod in my direction is loud as the car horn.

Doubly dismissed. "Fine. I'll go sit in the hall."

In one stride, Jayce is sliding open the glass, pointing at the balcony. "It's beautiful out."

Why not? Do they think I won't hear them on the other side? I walk into the sunshine and the door slides closed with a click. The view is amazing. The street below us is narrow, just like I imagine the streets Amber is walking in Europe. I wish I could call her, but I know she isn't traveling with her cell.

The phone taunts me at the top of my open backpack. Troy's letter is underneath.

I haven't really forgiven him, but I'm desperate to talk to someone so I dial his number. "Troy?"

I can hear the smile in his "hello." My heart speeds from zero to sixty in one second flat.

"Beau, I'm glad you called."

I perch on a sleek chrome stool. "How's your dad?"

"Hold on." Rustling and scraping sounds whisper through the phone.

"What happened?"

"The doctors think he had a minor stroke. That's why he fell. They kept him at the hospital last night."

"That's great!" Great his dad fell? Great his dad had a stroke? Ugh, stupid! "Are you okay?"

"Yeah, just tired of listening to him complain about missing work. He's lucky he'll be fine."

I don't know what else to say, so I cop out and change the subject. "Mom's acting weird."

"Honest, we didn't sleep together."

Hearing him say it, I know it's true. "I believe you."

"Thanks."

I can almost feel his relief.

"Mom wore khakis yesterday and the day before she ate a burger!"

"She's going normal on you!"

I haven't thought of it that way. Troy makes me laugh about the craziness of my life.

I tell him about the rest of the trip: Mary and the Mississippi, the pervert and the policeman and the personal assistant. It's good to talk to him. To feel like I have a friend.

I'd forgotten about being excluded by Star and the Terminator until I hang up. No sound penetrates the heavy glass. It's probably bulletproof, too. But it is a window to some serious emotions.

Jayce stands with his arms crossed, while my mother points

toward me and makes gestures. Her meaning isn't clear. She would make a horrible mime.

Neither of them seems to notice I am watching. My mother is building toward something. I may not know what she's saying, but I've seen her escalate a conversation into an argument on numerous occasions: cheeks flushed, movements jerky.

He is winding up, too. A vein pulses beneath the brown skin at his jawline.

I do not want to see this giant man angry. After what happened last night, I will not let him touch her, no matter what she's saying.

Pound, pound, pound. Most glass would break by now. "Mom!" I shout, knowing she can't hear me. Jayce notices. He opens the door and asks my mom, "Does she know?"

I don't let her answer. "Yeah, I know. Life in the old days: sex, drugs, and rock and roll. Time to go, Mom."

She is already on her feet. "I'm sorry, Jayce."

His massive head shakes back and forth. "It's a lot to take in." He reaches into his pocket and throws something at me.

I catch it without thinking. A roll of cash, the outside bill a hundred.

My mother, her hand on the doorknob says, "Thank you."

We are out of the room, out of the office, out of the building and I am in the dark. "What was that all about?"

Star unlocks the car door and sits in the driver's seat. "We'll discuss it later."

I bite the cuticle on my thumb almost down to the knuckle. I don't want to wait, I don't want to argue, I want to scream.

Thirteen

Rolling down the highway, my muscles are as tight as the electric green rubber band wrapped around the roll of hundred dollars bills. Do I really want to know why he threw them to me?

I focus on the stiff paper under my fingers, Ben Franklin staring up at me. When I was a little kid, I wore sneakers with my toes poking out in the rain and sorted through bins at Saint Vinnie's for clothes. We had enough food, most of the time.

Who knew the trip would make me rich? First, the Oyster fund, then the bracelet money, and now this.

Rich enough to buy: a plane ticket home, a complete set of rapidograph pens – seven different points and twenty brilliant colors, my own tattoo machine. Bees of conscience buzz through my brain. "Why did Jayce give me the money?"

My mom's foot presses on the gas pedal. "I told him we needed it."

"But why did he throw it to me?"

A thought flashes through my mind, making my stomach clench. Oblivious to obvious in two seconds flat. "Does Mr.-I'm-in-charge-security-guy think he's my dad?"

Her shoulders lift and settle back into place. "Maybe."

"What do you mean maybe?" I shout. "Wait. Don't answer that."

This morphing has to stop. First Star to Elizabeth and now, maybe, Jimi to Jayce. "What about Dad and Miles and Grammie Rose?"

"They're still family."

"Maybe." I copy her voice with a twist of sneer. "Maybe we're not related!"

This is way too much change for one day.

My mother navigates us back to the highway. Silence. She answers me with silence. At least that is familiar.

I sit and stew as the miles and the hours roll by. How could she betray me? And then I understand. It's not about me.

It's about her.

Two and a half hours later we're crossing the Tappan Zee Bridge. My mom is shaking and I'm hoping the car doesn't sway into the other six lanes of traffic. "You drove across the Mississippi, what's the big deal?"

She takes a huge breath and holds it before saying, "This is closer to home."

Home? Westwood, Massachusetts is not my home. But I am jittery, too. For my mom, it's the known that's making her anxious. For me, the unknown.

The landscape whizzes by and I'm surprised that New York is woods and fields – like the land around Eugene. Listening to folks in Oregon, I'd thought the entire East Coast was skyscrapers, parking lots, and malls.

My mom turns off the radio. "There's something we need to discuss."

Here it comes, another monstrous secret.

She takes a deep breath. "I don't know if I've ever explained how different people are in New England."

"Not everyone in Eugene wears tie-dye and smokes pot, Mom."

She tries again. "It's not the same. The pace is much faster, people are less friendly."

"So?"

She ignores the interruption. "The expectations are different, they're stratospheric compared to Eugene."

When did my mother start using advanced placement vocabulary? Who cares what worries people in Westwood?

Ten minutes later she turns off the highway into a huge, half-filled parking lot surrounding an enormous mall. My eyes narrow.

Memory: begging for money to go to the mall with Amber and buy some clothes for my thirteenth birthday. Star refusing, insisting we were not going to support the corporate machine that enslaves workers forcing them to destroy the planet's environment. And all I wanted was a new pair of jeans.

Places change. People change. Parents should not change.

"We're going to the mall?" I ask. "What about the evil corporate giants taking over the earth?"

She turns on her fish-eye stare. "They're clothes, Rainbeau."

An argument presses against the roof of my mouth. Wait. Why am I arguing about going to the mall?

We stroll through the stores, my senses on overload: the nauseatingly sweet scent of perfume, people swarming by, a display of jewel-tone jerseys. Who'd want a sweater in June?

A few cool minutes later, teeth chattering and skin shivering, I'm ready to buy one. To go with the jeans I'm considering. With hundreds of dollars in my pocket, purchasing power courses through my veins.

My mother approaches with an armload of khaki.

"I will not wear those."

"Yes, you will," she says and marches toward the dressing room.

When did my mom become the mall clothes Nazi?

Together we squeeze into a space the size of a closet, a small closet.

"A skirt, Mom. Really?" When I refuse to take it, I'm surprised by the look of desperation in her eyes.

"You must. Your grandmother…"

My fingers curl toward my palms, the tension of my clenched fists travels up my arms and out my mouth. "Yeah, she's sick. But I've given up my friends, my plans, my summer for this stupid trip. Now you want me to look like Freaks R Us! Forget it!"

My mother blocks the exit, preventing me from storming out of the tomb-sized space. "Please, Rainbeau. Your grandmother is dying." Her hands clasp as if in prayer. "How you're dressed when you meet her will mean a lot to her. To me."

Anger overflows the walls I had carefully built to contain it. "What about when I had pneumonia? The doctor said I could die. Did she even call? No."

Star slumps against the wall. "She had her reasons."

I snort. It is not a pretty sound. "She didn't even bother to call on my birthday — ever. Why should I care what she wants? Why do you?"

"Your grandmother's dying of cancer. She paid for the trip. We slept in motels."

"Right! Like the one with the pervert? I paid for Troy's ticket and Sergeant Security gave me the money. I'll buy what I want!" This discussion is as over as last month's pop star. I reach across her and push open the door. I am out of the room and out of the store.

The fountain in the mall is spewing chlorinated sparkles. I sit on the edge and wonder what kind of coin it would take to change my life. The mist surrounding me could be steam, I am so mad.

Star plops down beside me and I realize she is still in her pajamas. Her face has that droopy, Bassett hound look.

It occurs to me. "You're the one who wants new clothes. Who needs new clothes."

Her voice is almost too tiny to hear, "I don't think it will matter."

I drag her back to the khaki clothing corner. While she's trying stuff on, I pick out jeans and tops. There is not a single bathing suit on the entire floor. When I finally find a salesperson, I ask, "Where are the bathing suits?"

"Dear, it's June!" She waddles away.

In Eugene, June is summer, people swim, they wear bathing suits. And why is this different on the East Coast?

It's after five when we finish shopping. My mom eats an ice cream cone for dinner. I take a chance and order a banana strawberry smoothie, no yoghurt.

"It's only three and a half hours to Westwood. We can get there tonight." My teeth tighten against each other. If I could suck the words back in, I would. I am not ready to arrive at our destination.

"No. No, it's too late. We can be there in time for lunch tomorrow."

Tonight, I choose the hotel. With a pool instead of a pervert. By eight o'clock, we're both asleep.

The next morning we're up early, quietly getting dressed, skipping breakfast. My stomach does a cramp dance and I don't know whether it's hunger or nerves. I am hoping for frequent rest stops along the interstate.

The highway cuts diagonally across Connecticut. In Massachusetts we merge from I-84 onto I- 90. I try to calm myself by creating new flash designs in my mind, but all I imagine are frogs in bathing suits.

Three thousand miles and a billion hours on the road, but it is these last few minutes that I am the most antsy.

Will my grandmother tell me why she's ignored me for fourteen years? Will she accept me? Will she love me?

I rub my tattoo across my lip, try not to bite my cuticles, and fail.

My mom's mouth presses into a grim, thin line. Her fingers

grip the wheel, reaching the white zone for the first time since driving on the mountain roads in Oregon.

If Grandmother doesn't want us, we can always go home.

Goosebumps flashmob my skin. What if my mom isn't planning on returning?

I tune into her mid-sentence. "...snooty. It isn't like Eugene at all and your grandmother, I don't even know where to start."

The cotton khakis feel stiff under my fingers as I pat her leg. "It'll be fine, Mom."

And then I realize that is wishful thinking. My stomach tightens. My flesh prickles. I sound just like her.

She takes a deep breath and doesn't say anything.

Westwood looks like all the other small New England towns we've seen from the highway: a few old houses, some cute cottages my mom calls Cape Cods, and plenty of mud-colored split-levels.

The only unusual thing is the stoplights at almost every intersection. "It's strip malls and gas stations. What's with the attitude?"

She takes a left turn. "Just wait."

A few blocks from town, acres of land surround McMansion after McMansion. Each one big enough to house an entire commune from Eugene.

Driving on a dirt road, we bump along passing one home with two tennis courts and another with both an indoor and an outdoor pool.

A humongous hole in the road slams me into the seatbelt. "Why isn't it paved?"

"It's private. The people who live here prefer to discourage people from driving on it."

Foot wiggling, maybe I have to pee or maybe I don't. "How much farther do we have to go?"

My mom turns left and her attempt at a smile is a complete failure. "We're here."

"It's another unpaved road, Mom."

We rattle along. Maybe the old Subaru will leave pieces behind, like bird-proof breadcrumbs, so we can find our way back.

"No, it's the driveway."

White and pale gray stones crunch under the car wheels. The woods on the left are moss and forest and hunter green. Neatly manicured shamrock pastures stretch out on the right, separated by white board fences.

This? This is her home? In Eugene, when our food stamps ran out, we went dumpster diving. My eyes prickle with holding back tears of frustration. "Mom, how could you live in the yurt after growing up here?"

We move forward between the giant oaks lining the drive, a living tunnel leading to the front door. "It just happened."

Sparks of resentment ignite. Poverty was her choice!

My head pounds, thumping in rhythm to the angry beating of my heart. The tension in the car rises ten degrees with each turn of the tire. The blood on my thumb leaves a metallic taste on the tip of my tongue.

Angry words hurl themselves at my lips. I look at my mom and bite them back before they escape.

Worry creases the skin by her eyes. She nibbles at her lower lip to keep it from quivering. My mom looks so fragile, one harsh word and she might crack.

I force my feelings into the pit-of-no-return, hoping it isn't already full.

The three-story white-washed brick house looms over us as we step out of the Subaru. One person lives in all that space?

My mother winds her hair into a bun. I resist the urge to reach over and tuck a strand behind her ear. She forces a bare curve to her lips, an I'm-not-happy-to-be-here smile. "Ready?"

Slate-blue sky, ash-gray stone. I gaze anywhere but in her eyes where the pain is palpable. A shadow moves behind a sheer snowy curtain on the second floor.

"Rainbeau, there's something I haven't told you about your grandmother."

In that moment, I have the crazy notion that my grandmother is hideously disfigured, the evil witch in a fairy tale.

My mother grasps my hand. "I'm not sure how to tell you this."

Eyes darting from the house to my mom, I ask, "What?" Finally, answers and explanations!

I hold my breath and focus on the nervous look in her blue eyes.

"She's a conservative."

If my mother didn't look so morose, I'd laugh. Politics! I'm concerned about whether or not my grandmother will accept me as family, particularly since there are fourteen years of evidence to the contrary. Or perhaps, lack of evidence since my grandmother hasn't ever acknowledged my existence. And my mother is worried about who the woman voted for in the last election.

Fourteen

I follow my mom down the flower-lined walkway. The sweet scent of lavender and roses evokes a grandmotherly image: gray hair, dimples, a welcoming smile. Baking cookies in an oven, and not the kind for disposing of candy-fattened children. The trip down imaginary lane lasts only a moment.

The door opens inward before my mom can ring the bell. "Good morning, Hawkins."

My mother is talking to a butler. Like it's normal to have servants. We step in, the door closes behind us, and there is Hawkins: a tall white man with graying brown hair, round glasses, jeans, and a button-down shirt.

"Welcome home, Elizabeth. Your mother is in the garden room."

Is a garden room the same as a greenhouse?

A spiral staircase, high ceilings, and a confusion of doors

make me feel like Alice in Wonderland.

My cuticles are non-existent, but I bite the raw skin anyway. Now I'm agitated and I'm in pain.

Lining the walls are old-fashioned oil paintings of horses with tall, thin legs and short tails. I shake my head at the poorly proportioned animals and the clack of the beads on my braids threatens to announce my arrival. I still them and a shiver of anticipation shoots down my spine.

We enter a room with two shiny black grand pianos, their curves fitting together like pieces of a puzzle. Musical instruments I've never seen before hang from the ceiling. I stand there, my mind fills with images for flash, barely registering where my mom is headed. I stumble to catch up, crossing the room, which is larger than the entire yurt.

I expect a quivering voice, a small woman wrapped in a shawl, the smell of old people. Instead an irritated, arresting voice says, "I know we're short-staffed, just walk the damn horse and I'll be down soon." A phone clicks. "Elizabeth."

"Hi, Mom."

I hesitate in the doorway of a room filled with plants and wicker chairs. Leaning forward, just a little, I see a desk covered with papers. A woman sits there. Her back is muscular and rigid, her hair short and gray.

My mother perches on the edge of a flowered cushion, her knees clasped together and the toes of her new shoes pointing toward each other. "How are you feeling?"

Before answering, my grandmother swivels in her seat and sends a text. "Fine." She runs her fingers through her hair. "Except for the patchouli, which I can smell from here."

138

Gurgling, my stomach complains about missing breakfast or maybe missing the grandmother I'd imagined. This is no cookie baking, loving, dying grandma.

My mom smoothes the oxford shirt tucked into her khakis. "There is something I need to tell you."

Bony fingers organize papers on the desk. "Out with it, I've got a new horse colicking. The chit chat can wait."

My mother curls forward, arms crossed against her chest. Her words are hesitant, halting, "I brought my daughter with me."

"What?" My grandmother explodes off her chair. Papers fly through the air. "A daughter! Who is she? Where is she?"

I implode, shrinking smaller and smaller until I am on the floor hugging my backpack, holding my breath.

My mother never told her. No phone calls, no birthday presents, no wonder.

My mom is pleading, guilty, "Rainbeau."

"What the hell kind of a name is Rainbow?" my grandmother yells.

I force myself to stand, swaying, light-headed. There is one step down into the garden room and I hover on the threshold. My voice is lost somewhere deep inside me.

My mother motions for me to enter the room saying, "This is Rainbeau Louise Harley."

My mouth twists in a grimace. She could have just introduced me as Rainbeau or Rainbeau Harley.

Grandmother turns and glares at me, gaze harsh above a hooked nose.

"This is your Grandmother Louise."

We are in a lockdown-take-no-prisoners staring contest. Hazel-green eyes to hazel-green eyes, Louise to Louise.

She is a hawk moments before it pounces on a mouse. Clicking her tongue, she spins her finger in a circle, motioning for me to rotate.

But I am no mouse and no toy poodle.

I am white, hot fury. Motionless, I glare.

"Sullen?"

Rage erupts into words. "Sullen is not the same as angry."

Grandmother waves her hand dismissively. "Well, at least you have some guts. Which is more than I can say about your mother."

I was given a compliment at my mom's expense. I'm furious with her, but it feels like the mauve and cream oriental carpet has been pulled out from under me.

Grandmother Swift raises an eyebrow at her daughter. "Well?"

My mother looks like glass that has cracked, but hasn't yet fallen to pieces.

Flaming fury fades into midnight rejection. I will not listen to my mother's excuses.

They will not see me cry. I rush toward a riot of color, out the glass door and into the garden: dark blue delphiniums, red-violet roses, deep pink dahlias.

Before me is a wall of evergreen as high as the first floor of the house. I cross the flagstone patio, the muted grays and browns complementing the cushions on the wrought iron furniture. Stepping through an arched entrance neatly carved from the green boughs, I enter a maze, like those in a storybook with a castle and an evil grandmother.

Tears flowing, nose running, I collapse on a stone bench. All those hours in the car I'd built up hope that when we arrived I'd have a real family.

Why did I think my grandmother would be any less selfish than my mom? Selfish. Shellfish. At least Oyster isn't here.

My sobs subside and drying tears prickle my cheeks. I let myself get lost in the greenery. Focusing on the beauty surrounding me. Wandering, wondering at sculptures of warriors and horses and angels.

I turn a corner and an exit appears. An archway, outlined in evergreen and cornflower blue sky, framing fields and an enormous barn.

Stepping amid the gently swaying grasses, a whooshing noise sounds and there is a slight tremor beneath my feet. Behind me three gigantic, slobbering monsters charge in my direction.

My legs are moving before my brain says, run! The knee-high plants prevent me from sprinting. The hunters are howling and I am their prey. I trip and scramble to keep moving, my pack banging against my back. The barn is too far away.

A dozen steps and they are on me, bringing me down. Sprawling on the ground, I curl into a ball. Fear tightens its grip on my throat and my heart. Worse than the Oyster attack. I steel myself against the vicious bites, tearing flesh, and red, red blood.

That never come.

I force one eye open. Three labs. Black, brown, tan hairy bodies press against me. Moist tongues lick and wet noses poke. Sharp nails scratch and heavy tails thump.

Sitting and surveying the non-damage, I conclude the beast

bombardment is all woof and no tooth. "Enough! Can't you tell I'm not a dog person?"

The brown one sits three inches in front of me, tongue hanging out, panting. Eww! Dirt and dead things – dog breath. The blonde one is on its back and even I know it's asking for a tummy rub. The black one is sniffing around by my feet. A grasshopper pops out and lands on its nose. The dog's eyes cross as it tries to look at the intruder.

Laughter bubbles up inside me and when it escapes the bug leaps to freedom. The black runs around chasing after it. I scratch the blonde's stomach and its leg beats the ground as if it's trying to jump-start a motorcycle. The brown sticks its nose in my face and licks the salt from my cheeks. Amber would be so proud of me!

Danger past, the thought I've been avoiding rises up to confront me: My mother never told my grandmother I existed. A waterfall of sad slides down my face, releasing a moan.

I hug the brown dog and it wriggles closer, soft eyes seem sympathetic. I sob into its fur. It sits as I cry as if calming teenagers is its purpose on earth. My heart, weighing as much as the dog beside me, heaves as I hiccup.

The dog licks my snotty nose, which is gross, but convenient. It must be getting its yearly saline supply. I check her tag. "Thanks, Nutmeg."

The tan dog is begging again. When she rolls onto her back, it's easy to read the name on her collar. "Hey, Ginger," I say as I rub her belly.

Grasshopper dog comes over to check out the petting scene. "Sit." Surprisingly, she does. "Good dog, Pepper."

Now that we've made friends, they run off to find some other sad, sobbing teenager. I rub my thumb across my tattoo. Troy won't believe I've been comforted by dogs.

A nicker fills the air. Following the sound, I find two horses in a small fenced area. A large gray is grazing, while a small black is standing by the fence, ears up, eyeing my approach.

I don't know much about horses. Except they like sugar and carrots and I don't have any.

The black stretches its neck toward me. I've upped my animal bravery quotient thanks to the dogs. Avoiding the horse's head and those very large teeth, I tentatively pet the hair on its back. Its coat is softer than I expected.

The dogs have returned, milling around my ankles. The horses ignore them. "You're used to each other, aren't you?"

I close my eyes. Fear and fury fade away. I settle into myself and the calm from the horses seeps into my soul. Peace flows through me, washing away the anger.

Bees buzz in a nearby bush. For once, I am not afraid. The dogs run off again, their motion a ripple on the surface of a deep pond. I am the depths, soaking up the warmth of the moment.

A voice, full of dust and gravel intrudes, "She likes you. Usually, it takes her a while to warm up to someone new."

Startled, I find myself staring at a man almost straight in the eyes – someone my size. His brown, wrinkled, open face looks familiar. It takes me a moment to realize he is in the photo with my mom that I snuck a peak at a lifetime ago. "Who are you?"

I realize how rude that sounded and try again. "Sorry. I'm Rainbeau."

He sticks out the thick, calloused hand of a man who's no desk jockey, grabs mine, and shakes it hard. "Jones."

Is he laughing at me? "Just Jones?"

"Too small for a big name." He runs his fingers down the black's face and touches his nose to the white snip between the horse's nostrils. "I'm the barn manager. And you are?"

"I'm Star...Elizabeth's daughter."

"Daughter? Well, won't Lou be surprised."

Lou. The short name fits my short-haired, short-tempered grandmother.

He scratches the gray between the horse's ears. "She's been talking about your mom's return for days, odd she never mentioned you."

"My mother never told her about me." My words are soft as the swishing grass. I reach for the comfort of the horse's back, but she turns her head toward me instead. I will myself to stay still, hoping she won't bite. Instead, gentle lips explore my hand.

Jones says, "I guess it didn't go so well."

I stroke the silky white snip on the black's nose and frown. How can I divulge my feelings about my grandmother to someone who works for her?

"I've known her since we were kids," he says. "Worked for her for forty years. Your grandmother's a tough old bird."

"No shit." The words have flown out and there is no way to take them back. I cover my mouth, ignoring the fact that my hand is coated in horse slobber.

Jones laughs, a hee-hawing sound that makes me smile. "No shit. Yup. That's exactly how she is. Let me guess — you are, too?" He settles his lean, muscled forearms on the middle fence rail and fiddles with a piece of hay. "What happened?"

I hesitate, but there is nothing about his stance or his look that is judgmental. "She said I was sullen. I told her there is a difference between sullen and angry."

"Whoowee!" he shouts, startling the horse. "She's gonna have her hands full."

He motions for me to follow him and starts walking toward the barn. Up close, it is an enormous two-story tan building. I have been brave with Nutmeg and Ginger and Pepper and even braver with the black horse. I take a chance and ask, "Can I see the new horse, Collie King?"

His quizzical look makes me wonder what mistake I've made now.

"Collie King?" His voice arches upward on the last syllable.

"Grandmother said she has a horse, Collie King, so there wasn't time for chit chat."

Lip wiggling, cheek twitching he sucks back a laugh and says, "Oh, colicking. That's when a horse's intestines get plugged up. If they roll, the guts twist and it can be fatal."

"Just walk the damn horse." My grandmother's words, not mine. The impersonation is good enough to hear Jones's donkey bray laugh again.

With a horse about to die, it doesn't seem like a good time to be joking.

He reassures me with a smile. "Don't worry. The new horse is fine."

We walk into the cool, dark barn. It smells of animals and hay and I have an odd sense that I am home. A sense that life has changed. A deep breath, air filling my lungs, muscles relaxing, a sense that I've changed.

Jones and I are quiet together.

Then a horse whinnies and another kicks the wall.

Jones shushes them and turns to me. "If you haven't realized by now, I'll let you in on a well-known secret: You're Grandmother's a bit of a drama queen."

A bell rings. Eight notes in a familiar pattern that I cannot place.

"You better get back to the house," he tells me. "She doesn't take kindly to people being late to lunch."

The question is: Do I care?

Fifteen

The driveway winds between the pastures from the barn to the mansion. I trudge along and consider eating the nut-free, gluten-free, taste-free bar in my backpack, but things are already bad enough with my grandmother. I don't want to make it worse if there's a chance I can convince her to send me home. I don't think I have enough of the Jayce cash left to pay for a ticket and she can definitely afford one.

I shuffle up three steps onto a small deck. Herbs arranged in cedar boxes spice the air. On the other side of a sliding glass door is a plump woman in a salmon-striped apron bustling around an enormous kitchen.

When she stops to blow wisps of gray hair off her damp forehead, she notices me and opens the door. "Well, my dear, you must be Rainbeau. I'm Mrs. Hawkins."

The cook and the butler are married. My grandmother does

live in a fairy tale. Does she keep a magic mirror on the wall or will I have to clean out the fireplaces?

"You'd better hustle and wash up, dear. Madame," she winks at me, "won't be happy you're late."

I approach one of the three sinks in the kitchen. Mrs. Hawkins flaps her elbows in a fair imitation of a flustered hen. "Not in my sinks, you don't. Use the bathroom next to the mudroom."

She shoos me toward a yellow door. Nearby is a room with coats neatly hung on pegs, boots lined up below. Not a speck of mud to be seen.

Hands clean, I pick up a platter of melon slices on the counter.

Mrs. Hawkins nearly drops a pitcher of lemonade. "Put that down!"

She definitely takes the servant thing too far. I do as I'm told and follow her down a hall and around a corner.

My grandmother and mother sit at opposite ends of a long, lace-covered table in a room brightly lit by a wall of windows. The family matriarch extends a bony arm, one finger pointing to an empty seat. "You're late."

"No shit" I think. It is my new phrase.

My grandmother's voice booms, "Did you wash your hands?"

"Yes." Does she think I'm five?

Mrs. Hawkins offers me a plate of sandwiches. "No, thank you." At least she isn't serving oysters.

Grandmother Swift leans forward in her chair, "Tell me about yourself."

I hate that question. You either sound like your boasting or your stupid.

School first. "I'm a B student." I don't mention the minus.

"Why not an A?"

I have no idea how she wants me to answer, so I opt for honesty. "I don't work hard enough. There are other things that interest me."

She nods her head as if she understands, but doesn't stop the grilling. "Such as?"

"Tattoos."

She chokes on her Caesar salad, spluttering, "Tattoos?"

My mother jumps in, but her defense is many moves too late. "She's a talented artist."

My grandmother's eyes widen. "Tattoo artist?"

"I'll have my own shop after I get my BFA. Owners can make as much as a doctor or a lawyer." There. That should satisfy her.

She taps on the table. "I see."

But my grandmother doesn't see anything at all. She might as well be wearing a horse's blinders. She doesn't understand the tattoo shop is the only safe place I have and Uncle Miles is the only family who truly cares about me.

Her voice saccharine sweet with a bitter edge, "My dear, you are going to have to adjust to the fact that there is a new world order. This world does not include tattoos. You are no longer living in a hippy hovel where anything and everything goes."

"I don't want to be here." My voice hardens, "You don't want me here. Why not send me home?" The words more command than question.

My grandmother is the queen of commands. "That is not an option."

Dejection surrounds me like a cloud of insects.

Folding her napkin and placing it by her plate, my grandmother continues, "This is my house and you will abide by my rules. Including being punctual for meals and having a seemly hairstyle."

My hand sweeps through my braids, rattling the beads.

She turns to my mother and says, "We're going riding."

My mom fiddles with the food on her plate. "Rainbeau can't go."

"Nonsense."

"She's afraid of animals."

"That's ridiculous!" Grandmother glares at me. "Fine. Elizabeth, meet me in the tack room in half an hour. We'll find you some breeches and boots." She leaves her salad half-eaten and sails out of the room.

How can I explain to them that my feelings about dogs and horses have changed? Then it hits me as if I've been run over by four hooves and twelve paws. I can't and even if I tried my mom wouldn't listen. The best I can do is to go back to Eugene.

I suck in a deep breath and bite the hard cuticle on my middle finger. "Mom, I didn't know you rode."

Stacking dirty dishes on a tray, Mrs. Hawkins says, "Your mother was a champion. Her ribbons are still hanging in the den. Didn't she tell you about it?"

"She doesn't tell me anything."

Mrs. Hawkins harumphs out the door.

My mother pushes an anchovy to the side of her plate. "Why

couldn't you just agree with your grandmother?"

"Why should I? She's a mean old …"

"Rainbeau!" Her voice is firm, the change startling. "She's your grandmother."

"She doesn't act like one."

My mother waves her hands to encompass the entire estate. She knocks into her water glass and it rocks, wetting the tablecloth. "Your grandmother has so many responsibilities: the staff, her horses. She wasn't always there for me when I was a girl, but at least I was respectful."

The volume of my voice cranks a few notches. "You mean scared."

Her fingers tremble and her face pales. "She loves you, just like I love you."

Fourteen years of anger escapes. "You never loved anyone but yourself. Same as Grandmother."

A tear drips down my mother's nose. Words come, as soft as they are unconvincing, "I do love you."

"Why don't you defend me? Why don't you think about what I need? Why do I always have to save you?" I pound my fist on my thigh, each question a door to so much more.

She dabs her runny nose with a linen napkin and says, "Don't you remember me in the hospital with you when you were two and ate a peanut? What about all the special meals I made for you for school?" She bites her lip and stares at her plate.

I remember Miles taking me to the emergency room. My mother showed up later, high as usual. And I've been making my own lunch since kindergarten.

I charge out of the room straight into Mrs. Hawkins. "Easy girl," she says, gently holding my arms.

Body stiff and cheeks hot, I will have to remember that in this house other people listen to your conversations.

"Would you like to see your room, dear?"

Curiosity the cat strolls through me chasing away the rats of anger.

My mother joins us, stepping more quickly as we follow the housekeeper who winds her way down the long halls and up the spiral staircase. A niche in the wall has a bust I am guessing is of my grandfather. I don't ask because how can I admit I don't know what he looks like?

At the top of the staircase, my mother rushes past us into a brightly painted bedroom. She grabs a pillow off the bed and twirls around. "Oh, Mrs. Hawkins! She didn't change a thing!"

I cross the threshold into periwinkle: floor, ceiling, walls. A bright yellow canopy hangs over the bed and sunflowers are everywhere: in a cobalt vase, trim on a mirror, stitched onto the pillows on the rocking chair.

Star runs her hand down a framed painting. "The Van Gogh *giclée* is still here!"

Mrs. Hawkins fluffs the pillows on the bed. "The room looks just as it did the day you left. Your breeches are still in the drawers."

My mother reaches for a photo on the dresser. "I...it's him." With shaking hands she shoves it toward Mrs. Hawkins. "Please take this away."

She slides it into her apron pocket before I can get a peek.

"Come with me," the housekeeper says. "I'll show you your room."

152

As we leave, I hear my mom whisper, "Home."

This mansion will never, ever be my home.

We pass six pastel-colored bedrooms and four bathrooms. Reaching a tall, heavy door, Mrs. Hawkins uses her weight to pull it open. I step through, thoughts of dungeons flickering through my mind. The narrow, windowless hall darkens as the door slams shut. Wall sconces throw little light on the deep green-patterned wallpaper.

She opens a door and motions for me to enter. "I thought it best if you stayed in this room, dear. Away from your grandmother, at least until she gets used to you."

The servant's quarters. Children shouldn't be seen or heard.

A note of apology sounds in Mrs. Hawkins's voice. "I'll be downstairs if you need anything."

It is the same size as my room in the yurt, about the size of the bed in my mother's periwinkle paradise, but I don't mind. It's cozy, comfortable, almost familiar. I open the tiny wooden drawers on the wall to the left of the door, counting seventy-eight. Most are empty. A few hold thimbles and needles, pins and spools of thread.

Amber tried to teach me to sew once. I had more holes in my hand than if I had used a tattoo machine.

The opposite wall, by the head of the bed, has one cupboard. Three steps and I cross the room and open it. An ironing board drops out with a bang. I jump sideways and my knee brushes a soft, peach-colored blanket on the neatly made cot.

The best part of the room is a window with a cushioned seat and a view of the fields and the barn. I settle in, sip on my almost empty water bottle, nibble my free-of-everything-that-tastes-good bar, and read a chapter in my novel.

When I look up from *The Blue Girl*, a sunbeam highlights the weathervane on the barn that is poking above the trees. It's still a beautiful day and I don't want to spend it in a sewing closet.

Maybe Jones could tell me some stories about my mom. I discover the back stairs that lead to the kitchen. The empty kitchen.

A cobalt glass bowl filled with Granny Smith apples sits on the counter. I grab one, wash it carefully, and take a juicy bite.

Slipping through the sliding door, I jog down the steps, my backpack bouncing. Gravel crunches under my feet. When I enter the barn, twelve heads of various shades of white, black, and brown turn to inspect me.

The earthy scent of leather lures me into a small room filled with horse paraphernalia. Jones is seated on a trunk in the corner polishing a pair of tall, black boots. "You just missed them."

I shrug, planted in the doorway until he motions me to a box nearby.

He nods, brushing the toe of one boot. "Lou and Liz are on the trails."

"Who?"

"Louise and Elizabeth"

Oh. Grandmother and Mom.

Convoluted strips of black leather hang by my seat. They're slick and oily beneath my fingers. "Does Grandmother own all these horses?"

"No. There are plenty of boarders."

"I thought maybe they were my grandfather's."

He buffs a boot with a rag. "Your grandfather died when your mother was twelve."

My cheeks are uncomfortably warm. I'd bite my cuticles, but they're all horsey.

"Your grandfather and grandmother rode together. She gave it up for a while after his accident, but she loved the horses too much to stay away forever."

"Accident?"

His glances at me, eyebrow cocked in surprise. "They were at a Thanksgiving foxhunt. Your grandfather was about to jump a stonewall when his horse stepped in a hole. The bay broke his leg and had to be put down. Your grandfather's helmet hit the ground and his head hit the wall."

"Was grandmother with him?"

Jones picks up the other boot. "No, she was in the back of the pack, fighting her ornery mare. He was dead by the time she arrived."

"What about my mom?"

"She was home. Your grandmother raised her pretty much on her own. With help from the Hawkins, of course." He puts the boots in bags and turns his attention to a large piece of black leather.

With the toe of my sneaker I trace a knot in the wood floor. "My mom never talks about family or horses."

"Either way, horses are in your blood."

"I don't think so."

I imagine Miles tattooing red and white ponies prancing around my arm like a tribal band.

Jones rubs a soapy sponge in circles across the leather. "You never know until you try."

"No thanks." A shudder shivers up my spine at the thought of climbing onto an animal that large. It's hard to believe my mother isn't afraid. Easy to believe my grandmother isn't. "Do you think she'll ever like me?"

His dark brown eyes focus on me for a long time. "I don't know," he says. "Maybe she has to get used to the idea of being a grandmother."

We're silent for a while. The deep, mysterious smell of leather and horses seeps into my pores and eases the tension from lunch.

Jones stands up and stretches. "Bring the apple core. It's time to get you started."

"On what?"

"Horses," he says. Walking down the aisle, I follow him. Large heads stick out of the doors we pass and each time I step aside.

Jones stops at a stall that, from where I'm standing, appears empty. "This is your mom's old pony who you met in the paddock. She's twenty-nine." He hands her a carrot. "Give her the apple. She'll love it."

I am not risking my fingers, so I drop it in the stall. "What's her name?"

"Well, your mom named her Rainbow Stardust, but we just call her Dusty."

"My mother named me after her horse?"

He does his cheek twitch, lip wiggle. "You could take it as a compliment."

Right.

"It could be worse. She could have named you after her dog."

156

Really.

"His name was Mud."

I laugh with Jones, wondering whether or not he is kidding.

He slips some leather straps over the pony's black head. "By the way, Dusty doesn't like the curry much."

"I thought they only ate hay and oats." His look tells me I've said something really stupid.

He grins, pink tongue poking between white teeth. "Good one! Only hay and oats."

This is not going to be easy. Maybe if I just listen, I won't make any more dumb mistakes.

It works. For the next hour, Jones talks nonstop about horses, horses, horses. I learn the difference between a curry brush and a soft brush, how to pick the muck out of a horse's hooves, that a saddle goes on their back and a halter and bridle go on their face. And just like little kids, too much sugar isn't good for them.

Dusty stands quietly with two ropes running from the halter on her head to the walls on either side of her. When I brush her, I can see over her back. I've learned that she's fourteen hands tall. At four inches to a hand, she measures fifty-six inches at the place where her neck meets her back – the withers.

My fear drains away with each stroke of the brush. Jones leaves me with her while he waters the horses. Trusting me, trusting the pony.

I pull over a stool so I can comb her mane, the stiff hair that goes up her neck. Leaning against her, she doesn't move at all. Before I think, I slide my left leg over her back.

I am on top of a horse!

Her muscles shift under my legs. Her hair is smooth and slippery. Her backbone pokes up under my butt. Now I know why people use saddles. I shift my weight to get comfortable.

Eyes closed, I revel in the feeling of power. Calm, confident, completely in control. This is why people ride.

A sharp-as-knives voice cuts through the air. "What are you doing?"

Dusty startles, backing away from my grandmother. I slide and grab the mane to steady myself.

"Get off that pony this instant!"

I would, if I knew how. The pony is no longer near the stool and all the yelling has agitated her.

Jones fast-walks down the aisle. He holds Dusty's halter and calms her with a treat. "Slide your right leg over her back, hold onto the mane, and lower yourself down."

My grandmother's onslaught continues. "What were you thinking? Don't you know anything? How could you be so stupid?"

Heart galloping, pony standing still, I do as Jones says. I risk a peek at him, but his mouth is puckered and his brows are straight, more worried than angry.

My throat is tight – her words are bony fingers squeezing me to silence. Blood speeds through my veins Thoroughbred fast.

The last word I hear in my grandmother's tirade is "Idiot!" My backpack in hand, I bolt out of the barn, past the paddocks, and plunge into the woods.

Sixteen

Each creak and hoot of the woods taunts screw-up, screw-up, screw-up. Every speck of happiness I scrounge, I screw up.

My grandmother could be proud of me for sitting on a horse. She could be happy to have a granddaughter. She isn't, so I will force her to get rid of me. Fast as a bucking bronc throws a cowboy.

I follow a small stream until it spills down a waterfall into a pool. My pack slips out of my fingers at the root of a willow. I collapse beside it. A lump of moss cushions my head and I search the celestial blue sky for signs of rain. Thunder and lightning, a hurricane – weather to match my mood.

No luck.

So I let my mind wander. Imagining a summer of working in the tattoo shop or sipping coffee in a Paris café or visiting Venus.

My body begins to relax. I will find a way to leave this place.

Snap! Crash! Snort! The brush erupts in sound and my heart stampedes. Are there bears in Massachusetts?

Chasing, racing dogs growl and howl. First, Ginger leaps on top of me and knocks me over. Nutmeg licks my face and I laugh until I smell poop.

"Ewe, gross!"

Pushing the dogs away, I wipe my face with my sleeve. "I am not a dog person."

In the front pouch of my pack is the hand cleanser. I squeeze the bottle until it makes a farting sound. While I rub my hands together, Pepper snatches it and races across the clearing.

"Come back here!"

She digs a hole, dirt flying behind her, drops the bottle in, and covers it up. Finished, she races toward me covered in dirt and drool.

Shaking my finger at her, I shout, "Plastic is not biodegradable!"

I am not going to dig up that bottle.

So, I won't get into recycling heaven. I imagine giant piles of trash needing to be sorted. Or is that recycling hell?

The slobber of dogs follows me to the house. Time for plan A: buck granny off my back.

There's no sign of anyone at the mansion, but it's so big who could tell? I leave the labs outside and enter the mudroom. The kitchen is empty, but it feels like I'm sneaking up the back stairs. Tip toe, tip toe. The only person I want to talk to is my uncle.

I don't need the phone number on the back of my Miles of Tattoos t-shirt. Even if it wasn't number one on speed dial, I memorized it back in the manfriend number four days.

Miles is probably working, but I really need to talk. I curl up on the window seat and call. "Hi! It's me."

"Hi, me!"

I don't mean to complain, but all my troubles pour out of me like a ketchup bottle that finally got unstuck. My voice is more four than fourteen. "I climbed up on a horse today and Grandmother screamed at me and the dogs gave me poopy kisses. I want to come home!"

"Hey, girl, I'm working. Remember the family motto: improvise, adapt, and overcome. I'm in the middle of a dragon. Gotta go. Love you."

Click.

Alone. Alone. Alone. Settles from my thoughts to my bones.

At least he answered. The family motto isn't my favorite, but we have one.

Do my mom and grandmother have a Swift family motto? It must be: Me Before Others.

"Improvise, adapt, and overcome." Maybe it's time to do a little improvising. If my grandmother doesn't like it, she can send me home.

I spend some time sketching miniature dragons, their bodies made up of the words from the motto. "Overcome" is the one shooting flames. I imagine tattooing them on my ankle, but I don't know if I could tattoo upside down, on myself.

There's a knock on the door. Before I have a chance to say it's okay, in walks my mom. She sits carefully on the cot and tucks her right foot behind her left ankle. "Can we talk?"

Why bother asking? I pull up my knees and cross my arms.

Her focus is out the window. "I know this is hard."

"Really."

"Your grandmother isn't always an easy person."

No shit. That phrase again. At least I didn't say it out loud.

"I tried to warn you."

"I get it. You're Mommy's perfect little darling who's finally come home. Perfect. Perfect. Perfect. Perfect, except for me."

She picks lint off the peach blanket. "It's not like that."

"Yes. It is." I pick up the phone, ready to speed dial Miles again. "Just send me back to Eugene."

My mother stands, her hand on the door. "Your grandmother has a plan."

"A plan? Like sending me home?"

"She and I will discuss it at dinner."

A niggle of doubt worms around my brain. "With me there."

My mom adjusts the shell barrette that has replaced her chopstick. "You'll eat up here."

"If the plan is about me, I need to have a say! Besides, all I've eaten today are protein bars!"

"You'll be fine." She slinks out the door. "Give it time with your grandmother. You'll get used to each other."

"How long are we staying? She doesn't even act sick!"

Questions hang in the air like Oregon mist.

My mother slips away. Her clothes may have gone conservative, but she's still clueless. My grandmother's dislike is chiseled in granite, with a jackhammer, for all the world to see except for the Star, Elizabeth.

An hour goes by while I color in the dragons and wonder what they will discuss. I work on a new design: the red and white ponies. Horses are way harder to draw than I had imagined. I use the eraser more than the pencils.

Someone pounds on the door and I jump off the window seat, heart thumping like Ginger's tail.

A warm voice says, "Rainbeau! Open the door please."

A sliver, a crack, pulled in until it touches the cot.

Mrs. Hawkins, arms loaded down with a tray, smiles at me. "Sorry I had to kick your door, dearie, I didn't want to spill your food." She sets it on the window seat and unfolds a tray table she had tucked under her arm. "You must be starving!"

A metal top covers who knows what allergenic catastrophes.

Caught between a rumbling stomach and a cautious nature, I blurt out, "I can't eat just any food."

"I know. It's carrot coriander soup." She places the tray on the table and takes the lid off. Steam rises from the bowl carrying smells spicy, exotic, and comforting.

Colorful cut-up vegetables: celery, cucumber, red and yellow bell peppers share the plate with a pork chop surrounded by orange nasturtium flowers. "Wow! I didn't know you could make food look this pretty."

Mrs. Hawkins smoothes her apron and beams an I'm-so-glad-you-noticed-smile. "Wait until you see the spreads for your grandmother's parties."

"How did you find out about my allergies?"

Her voice is smooth as hemp milk chai, "Oh, I have my ways." She winks and shuts the door.

All the food seems safe, though I've never eaten a nasturtium. I suck down the soup, listening for Mrs. H's steps as she goes down the stairs. The sound is faint, the vibrations take longer to stop.

When they do, I duck out of my room and pad down the hall barefoot. The heavy door separating the servant's quarters opens without a squeak. My breath comes short and shallow. Creeping toward the front stairs, slowly, slowly, descending. Senses on high alert, I guess the direction of the dining room.

I edge forward and see the pianos. My muscles hum, synchronized with the instruments hanging from the ceiling, stroked by invisible fingers. Before a full symphony plays along my skin, I rush out of the room.

Vague voices sound down a hall. Clearer, clearer as I draw nearer. Clearer until the words, distinct, halt my steps. Freezing my flesh, my bones, my heart.

Grandmother's voice is gravelly with irritation. "...solution. The child will go to Greyson."

Greyson. Only my mind functions, shifting through memory to discover where she plans to send me. Nothing.

No sound, but the scraping of silverware on china. Seconds pass, feeling like minutes, like hours. My peripheral vision darkens. I flatten myself against the wall and take one shallow breath.

My mother's voice is high-pitched and panicky. "Greyson? For boarding?"

Boarding? Like a dog at a kennel?

"Of course."

My chest aches, my heart splinters into fragments of ice. My legs begin a slow collapse.

Clatter. Pound. My mother shouts, "No!"

I stiffen, still standing.

"Mom, you can't." She is begging, not demanding.

"The child doesn't belong. If she had been raised here it would be a different matter."

My mother groans an anguished, animal sound. "Why do you think I didn't tell you about her?"

"Her" meaning me.

Hope evaporates leaving the salty grit of despair.

"I've wondered that since you arrived."

Moaning, my mom says, "I didn't want you to take her away from me."

My grandmother squawks, "As I would have."

I run, not caring if anyone hears my bare feet pounding on the wood floor. I run up the stairs to the servant's quarters. I run to the sewing room. It is not my room.

Grandmother's hatred overwhelms me.

Send me away?

No! No! No!

Sheets balled in my fists, I wake up having spent the night wrestling the bedcovers. A thought is sticky in my brain, like the residue in my mom's hash pipe.

I am not going to a kennel. I am going home.

My jaw pops with a huge yawn. I dress quickly and avoid the humming of Mrs. Hawkins as I head down the front stairs.

Out the door, to the barn, surrounded by the peaceful hug of the place. Can God be in a stable? Even I know the answer from preschool. His son was born there.

The pungent smell is strangely comforting, as if I'd grown up here. The horses munch on hay in their stalls. No one is in the aisles.

I poke my nose through a doorway. It looks like a living room filled with furniture and a giant picture window facing the woods.

Jones is on a stool, rag in hand, dusting some framed photographs. "How're you doing?"

I don't want to answer that. "Um, I have a question."

His tongue rolls across his lip. "Just one?"

"Well, it's really a favor."

He takes a picture off the wall and polishes it. "Shoot."

Maybe he doesn't want to help me. I shouldn't try. My idea sucks. But it's worth a chance if my grandmother gets so pissed off she sends me home. "Will you teach me how to ride?"

He shows me a picture of a girl about five years old, with blond braids. She is holding the reins of a white pony in one hand and a blue ribbon in the other.

There is something familiar about her. "Oh my gosh, is this my Mom?"

"Her first blue ribbon. She won it on a fat little pony named Dinky."

"She was way younger than me."

He re-hangs the picture. "Well, we better get started. You have some catching up to do!"

"I don't want my mom or my grandmother to know."

"A surprise. Great idea." He opens a closet door and rummages around, cursing.

Curious, I move closer and a piece of clothing flies toward me. I catch it and Jones hands me a pair of boots. "You can change in the bathroom around the corner."

I pull on the stretchy, thin, skin-tight leggings and smooth my hands down my very exposed thighs. My foot and ankle barely squeeze into a boot until I realize it zips up the back.

Do I look like the girl in the picture? In the mirror above the sink, I wrinkle my nose at my reflection. With my dark skin and beaded braids, there is no resemblance at all.

Jones has Dusty on the crossties, waiting for me. "I'll be back in twenty minutes," he says handing me a grooming box. "Brush her like you did yesterday."

He doesn't have to tell me not to get on her without him.

Starting at the pony's head, I work my way to her rump. I brush her body and legs twice: first with the hard brush and then the soft.

Jones returns, asking, "Why can horses jump so high?"

Lifting those huge bodies over a fence seems physically impossible. Will I have to jump Dusty today? I swallow a lump the size of a pony. Maybe I'm not ready for all this.

He scrapes the muck out of Dusty's hooves with a hoof pick. "Because they have frogs in their feet!"

I raise an eyebrow, skepticism pasted on my face. What do amphibians have to do with horses?

He rests Dusty's back leg on his thigh, pointing to the triangle in the bottom of the hoof. "This is called a frog."

"Why?"

"Why is a nose a nose?"

I counter, "Would a nose by any other name smell as sweet?"

Jones hands me a tail brush. "Girl, you and your grandma are two hackneys harnessed to a trap."

"Huh?"

"Matched ponies pulling a cart."

I'm a visitor to the horse world struggling with its customs and language. Too bad I won't be staying.

I stand way off to the side, brushing Dusty's tail, working through the snarls with my fingers. "Was that supposed to be a compliment?"

"It's a good thing," he says, picking up another hoof. "Maybe it's one of the reasons you two don't get along."

We don't have to. As soon as she sees me riding, she'll be sending me home to Eugene, home to the tattoo shop, home to Miles who is my family.

Jones carries an armload of leather. "This is an English all-purpose saddle." He places a white pad with the embroidered initials LES on the pony's back first.

I trace them with my finger, "LES?"

"Louise Elizabeth Swift, your grandmother's initials," He tightens a strap across Dusty's stomach. "This is a girth." Then he shows me how to put the thin straps of leather on her head, a bridle.

I imagine sun-on-my-face-wind-in-my-hair riding.

Jones hands me a hefty black helmet. Clamped on my head and strapped below my chin, I realize this may not be the safest way to get my grandmother to send me home.

He leads Dusty into the indoor ring. The patch of blue sky at the end of the aisle beckons.

"Aren't we going outside?"

"Learn to control your horse first, then you can ride out there."

With Jones's help, I scramble onto the saddle. He shows me how to hold the reins and attaches a very long rope to the bridle.

"It's a lunge line. This way, I control her."

I'd envisioned myself galloping across a field, not led around on a leash. As Dusty walks in a circle, a constant stream of instructions flows from Jones to me: sit up straight, heels down, straighten your back, feel her weight shift underneath you.

Don't the cowboys in the movies just hop on and go?

One of the grooms enters the ring and asks Jones a few questions. My muscles relax and I focus on feeling Dusty beneath me: her firm ribcage between my legs and the slight tug of her mouth on the other end of the reins.

"Okay," Jones says, "Are you ready to trot?"

As soon as the words leave his mouth, Dusty breaks into a bone-jarring gate. Gone are my feelings of comfort. I bounce hard, grab the mane in one hand and the saddle in the other and yell, "Stop!"

Dusty isn't inclined to listen.

"Easy girl," Jones says as he reels in the lunge line, making the circle smaller and smaller. "Push your heels down," he tells me.

When I do, my butt begins to swing in rhythm, up and down, up and down. I let go of the mane and just hold the saddle and she takes me around the ring bouncing, but not bucking.

I pull on the reins. "Whoa." Miraculously, Dusty slows to a walk.

We practice the transition from walk to trot and trot to walk for the next half hour. Every time I lose my balance, I scramble to grab the saddle or mane.

Finally, Jones says, "Ho," and Dusty halts without any help

from me. "Good job! How do you feel?"

I smooth the hair on Dusty's neck and avoid Jones's eyes. "The walk was okay, but the trot's awfully bumpy."

"You'll get used to it. In a few days you'll be posting like a pro."

I slide off, but my legs are too wobbly for me to care about a post.

"I'll put her away," Jones offers. "You might want to jump in the hot tub."

My grandmother has a hot tub? I doubt it's in the servant's quarters.

"Thanks, Jones."

He pulls the reins over the pony's ears. "Next lesson tomorrow." Dusty snuffles his collar, as if a carrot might be hiding there. "Six a.m."

My stomach slinks toward my backbone. If I am this sore now, what will tomorrow be like?

He looks at the clock hanging in the indoor ring. "You better scoot. Lou will be here any minute. We need to talk about a show coming up."

"She's not going to ride, is she?"

Jones snorts and the pony takes a step back. "Of course, she's riding. She hasn't missed this show since she was fifteen, forty-five years ago."

The blood pounds in my ears, making it hard to think. Doesn't Jones know my grandmother is dying?

My skin prickles. Amber said it means someone's walking on your grave. Or my grandmother's grave.

The pounding becomes a hum, filling my brain with sound.

He doesn't know. I take a breath, willing my blood to slow. "Isn't she dying?"

He stops in the aisle, his face hidden by the pony's thick neck.

An apology on my lips, I walk around Dusty.

Jones is past cheeks twitching, lips cracking. Seconds later, he is laughing so hard, tears course the canyons of his weathered face.

Dusty reaches out and blows softly in my hair. I straighten her mane, wondering what to do.

Jones stamps his cowboy boot on the rubber mat and spits into a stall. "Oh, girl!"

I slam my helmet onto a hook. No matter how nasty she is, my grandmother's impending demise is not a comedy routine.

Wheezing his way out of his laughter, he says, "She's not dying!"

I plunk down onto a pile of what I hope is clean shavings.

Jones squats next to me. "Haven't you figured it out yet? Your grandmother will do whatever it takes to get what she wants."

"She lied when she told Mom she was dying?"

I didn't have to make this stupid journey.

"Not exactly. She had a test done for cancer that showed up positive."

I stand and swat the shavings off my bum. "She has cancer?"

He cross-ties the pony. "She thought she did. The lab ran it a second time and it was negative. The report, the doctor exam, everything was negative. Turns out, she's in great shape."

"Does my mom know?"

Jones shrugs. "You'll have to ask her. She and Lou should be here any minute."

Finger to my lips, I say, "My riding, our secret."

He winks and starts brushing Dusty.

In the bathroom, I peel off the breeches. They should probably go in the wash, but I'm in a hurry. I roll them up, stick them in the boots, and shove everything in the closet.

I need time to think, to process, to plan. My grandmother is healthy, my mom's turned into a drug-free-conservative, and I'm stuck three thousand miles from home.

Seventeen

I miss the cool clear summer days of Eugene. Westwood is low gray skies and weather so humid everything sticks to your skin: shorts, grass, bugs.

The willow in the woods is my destination, but I only make it as far as the three birch trees. When voices murmur in the woods nearby, I fling myself onto a white scrolled bench, hoping the yellow-green leaves will hide me. The metal is cool and poky and hard.

My mom's laughter. Strange. Until I realize she hasn't laughed much, not on the trip, except for at Mary's, not since we've been living with the Slime.

They ride into view, my mother on a light reddish-brown horse and my grandmother riding a gray. I squish myself further, curlicues impressing themselves on my hips and shoulders. Peeking through the leaves, hoping they won't notice me.

The wind carries a snatch of conversation in my direction.

"…has a conference in Boston. Can Oyster, I mean Robert, visit?"

My grandmother answers, "Of course! I'll let Mrs. Hawkins know."

Oyster? Here? I am frozen in a fetal position, focusing on breathing. My eyes are shut tight against the possibility of not being safe here.

My mother and grandmother ride by and I realize I don't know when he is coming.

I have to get home to Eugene first.

If he is still angry, Grandmother and Hawkins and Jones will protect my mother. The truth is with them watching over her, she doesn't need me anymore.

After the crappy job I did while we were on the trip, maybe it's better that way.

I force my sore muscles into a sitting position. I'd pray to go home before Oyster arrives, but I have no idea where to begin. Prayer 101 wasn't taught in preschool.

By the time I arrive back at the mansion my stomach muscles have gone from clenched to complaining. Mrs. Hawkins has left a plate with sausages and peach slices on the kitchen table. I know it's for me when I see the sausage box with gluten-free written in large red letters. Servants preparing my meals. Since when did I become a fairy princess?

After I eat, I wash my plate and fork and dry them. Opening random cupboards looking for where they belong, I've never seen so many dishes. There's an entire set with Christmas trees on it. A set of dishes for one day of the year?

Grabbing a plum out of the fruit bowl, I pucker past the tangy tart taste of the skin as I walk up the stairs.

My cot is made, my clothes are neatly folded, and my novel is closed with a bookmark holding my place. Everything clean, tidy, neat and thankful is the last thing on my mind. So much for privacy.

A fresh shirt and shorts – no shower. I have no idea which one is the granddaughter-who's-being-sent-away bathroom.

I pad into the hall, the sisal rug rough and scratchy on my bare feet. The doorway across from my room is open. I gawk at the built-in bookshelves running floor to ceiling, filling virtually every space. Only a window, with its ubiquitous (my favorite Amber word) seat, remains free of neat rows of spines. Mr. Hawkins, in jeans and a Red Sox t-shirt, is standing by a small red leather couch that faces a fireplace.

"Hello, Rainbeau."

"Is this your room?"

"This is Mrs. Hawkin's and my study."

"All the books are yours?" My voice is filled with the wonder of someone who has spent a lifetime walking in the rain to the local library.

Hawkins's laugh is quick and light. "Why, yes. Though in truth some of them were your grandfather's, which he bequeathed to me. He and I shared many a glass of sherry discussing the swashbuckling of Long John Silver and the story of Jesus in the *Brothers Karamazov*."

I step into the room, bare toes curling into the thick maroon oriental carpet. All these stories would take a lifetime to read.

"You're welcome to borrow a book, but please ask Mrs. Hawkins or me first."

"Thank you!" No more two-mile walks. All I have to do is cross the hall. "Does Grandmother have a library?"

He straightens a few spines on a high shelf. "She prefers nonfiction, which she keeps in her office downstairs."

"Thanks." He isn't anything like I'd imagined a butler to be: stiff, silent, self-satisfied. The people who work for my grandmother seem to like her. She must be nice to them.

So why does she hate me?

Downstairs, I look for my grandmother's office. Maybe I'll find something to help me in my campaign to leave this place. My breathing quickens at the thought of being here when Oyster arrives.

Opening doors, I find closets near the kitchen and the dining room. Off the entrance hall, is a room lined with cabinets below paneled walls. A small fireplace has an old rifle resting on the mantle and a painting of, I'm guessing, my grandfather. Over the desk are three shelves filled with titles like: *The Tao of Equus*, *Dressage in the Fourth Dimension*, and *How to Bombproof your Horse*. Horses and bombs and different dimensions. Oh, my!

I bump into her open laptop and the screensaver pops up. It's the same photo I saw at the barn. The walls of the office are covered with pictures of my mom, my grandmother, and horses. And ribbons, lots of ribbons.

On the shelves above the desk, lined up in front of the books, are tiny horses under two inches tall: ceramic, wood, plastic. I choose the one that looks like Dusty. My grandmother must have forty figurines. She won't miss this one.

I hear voices on the front steps. My heart fast-trots and I tuck the miniature Dusty into my pocket. When I try to open the window, it doesn't budge.

There's only one way out of my grandmother's office. I am caught like a fox cornered by hounds. Nowhere to hide.

The front door thuds and my heart canters. My mother and grandmother are in the hall, discussing their ride.

What will they do when they find me? Greyson.

Steps move toward the office. Captured!

I need a reason for being in grandmother's office, all alone, with the door closed.

I do not have one.

The knob begins to turn. My mother's voice asks, "Can you show me that bit you mentioned?"

Grandmother answers, "This way. It's on display in the den."

Steps, two people's steps, tap down the hall and fade away. I wait for silence before tearing out of the office and up the front stairs to the sewing room.

Rain splatters my window as I plunk down on the seat. I wrap a soft blanket around my shoulders and snuggle up with Grammie Rose's afghan.

I think about my Grammie before she got cancer and died, about Miles, my dad, Jayce. Was my mom purposefully misleading Jayce so he'd give us money? Or does she really not know who's my dad?

I turn to my flash notebook. I can't control my genes, but I can control my drawings. The afternoon flows swift as a mustang across the plains as I sketch Celtic horses. The intricately woven strands take hours to perfect. When I finish, my eraser is worn to a nub.

The phone rings in a guitar riff – Troy.

"Hey! How's your dad?"

"Impossible to keep in bed." Troy's voice is pitched to a happy note. "He's already planning to go back to work."

"Wow, that's great!" Things are moving forward for Troy and his dad. I wish I could say the same about me and my mom.

"How's your grandmother?"

A number of unpleasant words run through my mind, all of them rhyming with 'itch'. "Okay, I guess." He has enough to worry about without me telling the truth. "I rode a horse today."

"Lucky! I miss riding. My uncle sold his ranch."

I rub my calf and the inside of my thigh. "It'll take a while to get used to."

Troy teases, "So you don't like dogs, but horses are okay?"

"There are three super-sized, slobbering labs here."

"Horses and dogs! How are you surviving?"

"It's not the animals —

"Hey, I've gotta go. I'll call you back later."

The phone flashes "end".

"—it's the people."

A couple more hours, reading and napping. I've skipped lunch again, not that anyone seems to have noticed. Maybe that's a good thing. They can forget I'm here. Until my riding is good enough to make my grandmother so angry she sends me home.

Tap, tap, tap.

Mrs. Hawkins did remember me. My growling stomach reminds me of the pork chop last night, that even tasted good cold.

My mom pokes her head in the room. "Hi!"

I stiffen, wondering if she'll mention "the plan", but I don't want to hear her explanations and excuses. They're on the bottom shelf of the last aisle in the satisfaction department.

"What?"

This time, she doesn't invite herself in. "I just wanted to let you know you'll have to eat with the Hawkinses tonight."

I bite the cuticle on my thumb, stop, and wrap my fingers around the injured digit. "Are you and grandmother having another big discussion or are you going to a ball?"

"A benefit, actually." She closes the door behind her, but quickly reopens it. "There's a yoga class at the barn this evening. You should try it."

"Yoga in a stable?"

"Yes, your grandmother says all the dressage riders do yoga or Pilates to stay in shape."

"The wicked witch does downward dogs?"

"Go to the class and try to fit in. You're good at yoga."

She's gone. To her ball or her benefit and I am Cinderella, left with the ashes.

One thing hasn't changed. She still doesn't answer my questions.

Dinner with the Hawkinses in the kitchen: buffalo tips sautéed in olive oil with green beans and diced red peppers. I haven't decided yet whether they are just being polite or they really are interested in my tat, my sketchbook, and my life.

Mrs. Hawkins glances over my shoulder. "Elizabeth, you look stunning!"

I almost choke on my chocolate tofu pudding. No one in Eugene would recognize my mom: a midnight blue sheath dress, matching heels, blond hair swept off her face with a beautiful butterfly clip. "Mom?"

She pats a stray hair into place with manicured fingers. "Very funny."

Mr. Hawkins stands and bows. "She walks in Beauty, like the night."

His wife pats his leg. "Thank you, Lord Byron."

My mom blushes. Painted lips part in a smile directed at Mr. Hawkins. "I need to go. Rainbeau please try the yoga class tonight."

Who knew? My mother really could be a fashion queen.

A whiff of perfume and she is gone.

"Mrs. Hawkins, who was in the picture my mom didn't want in her room?"

She throws a glance at her husband that is as clear as a brand-new tattoo.

"It was an old boyfriend of your mother's."

Mr. Hawkins adds, "Someone your grandmother wanted her to marry."

"Why didn't she?"

Mrs. Hawkins wipes her hands on her apron. "We don't know." She stacks dishes in the sink. "Your mother left suddenly, and we never found out why."

A family mystery and even the Hawkinses don't know the answer.

I help clear the table. "Thanks for dinner."

Mr. Hawkins, his hands covered in soapsuds, asks, "Are you

going to the class?"

"I guess so. It'll probably feel good to stretch."

I head upstairs to the sewing room to change. My yoga shorts are an old pair of Miles's boxers. There's a tiny tear in the butt, and there's a hole in my favorite tattoo t-shirt, but who cares? It's yoga in a barn, just how fancy could it be?

I head to the stable, the sticky evening air filled with flying, biting bugs. The giggles of a gabble of girls leads me to the upstairs viewing room. It is filled with seven pink, purple, and aqua clad teenagers, each in a different shade unitard with a yoga mat to match. The teacher, a sanctimonious frown pasted on her face, hands me a bright orange pad.

I may not look like the other girls, but I do know my yoga. I've been doing child's pose since I was a baby.

The instructor begins by having the girls attempt to sit in a semi-lotus position, chanting *Om*.

I flop down, pretzeling my legs into full lotus. "*Om mani padme om, om mani padme om…*"

The teacher is screeching, "New girl!"

My body is relaxing into the chant.

Except for the squawking of the instructor.

I settle inside myself. "*Om mani padme om.*"

"New girl!"

I crack open my eyelid. She is talking to me.

"Yes?"

Hands on hips, upper body tipped forward, the antithesis of calm. "It's om, not that gibberish you were moaning! Follow what we're doing."

Sheesh. I fit in as well here as Andre the Giant hanging out at the jockey club.

After a while, I forget the yoga shrew, the pastel parade, the horse smell. One pose flows to another. Even the familiar burn feels good.

At the end of class, the girls gather round to discuss what kind of pizza to order.

It seems an odd way to end a peaceful evening.

The teacher packs up, reminding us the next class will be in three days. She grabs the orange mat and leaves.

I consider following her until a girl with a light pink leotard and a short brown ponytail asks, "What do you like on your pizza?"

"Anything's fine." There is no way I am going to explain my allergies. If they want to treat me like I'm one of them. Why not? Maybe they won't notice if I don't eat anything.

Aqua-girl calls from her cell phone and someone pulls out a fashion magazine. They circle the table discussing the clothes in detail. Nauseating detail.

I am far more interested in an entire wall covered with my grandmother's ribbons and trophies. I spend the next half hour reading magazine and newspaper articles that feature her. My grandmother was even an alternate in the Olympics!

A girl in bright pink uses her reflection in the glass to apply lipstick. "What's your name?"

"Rainbeau."

"Right." Head cocked, hand on hip, smirk in place. "And I'm Fuchsia."

Okay. "You're named…"

"Fuchsia" shouts, "Hey, girls! Her name is Rainbow."

Aqua-girl asks, "Like Rainbow Brite?"

The girls snicker and someone calls out, "Is your pony's name Starlite?"

A girl in purple says, "My name's Violet."

"I'm Orchid."

"Pansy."

"No you're Periwinkle." They each choose a name to match their outfit.

This is so stupid.

The pizza arrives and the girls crowd around grabbing slices.

I'm out of here.

Aqua-girl, her blond ponytail swinging, calls out, "Rainbow Brite, here's a slice for you. Anything's fine, right?"

The last slice is piled high with toppings, including anchovies. I am not allergic to fish, just dough and cheese. I am not anaphylactic to either. I am not going to let Aqua-girl get the best of me.

I pick up the slice and take a large bite, smiling at my tormentors. One moment to enjoy the look of surprise on their faces before my throat begins to close.

Gasping for breath, lungs shrinking, fighting panic. Where's my epipen?

Aqua-girl laughs. "Don't you think you're overdoing it a bit?"

Violet waves a piece of pizza. "They're only anchovies."

Not oysters.

Faces swim. I am sinking.

Light pink, brown ponytail. "Where's her stuff? She's having an allergic reaction!"

Pastel palette blurs.

Sinking deeper. Fighting the abyss. Epipen?

Sweet smell of shampoo. Hard plastic in my hand. Strong fingers grasp mine.

Pow! Pain spreads through my thigh.

One… two… three seconds and I gulp air.

A male voice, "Back off!" Jones stabs my other thigh. "Lexie, call 911!"

Lexie, the light pink girl, says, "I did. They're on their way."

Air sucks past my ragged throat. Jones holds me gently. Time sways.

The paramedics arrive, all business and bustle.

"Granddad," says an EMT, "You can stay with her."

Jones holds me closer. "You'll be okay."

I wish he was my grandpa.

The ambulance and hospital are cold, bright, hard. Medicinal smells. People push and prod and poke.

"Mom?"

I need her.

Jones whispers, "I tried. Lou turned her cell phone off."

Needles, beeping lights, oxygen masks. In and out of consciousness.

I let go.

Eighteen

Jones lifts me out of the car, cradled in his arms, and carries me upstairs – so strong for someone so short. He lays me down on a giant cloud and sleep sweeps me away.

I wake up in a sunny yellow room surrounded by labs, two sprawled on the floor, a heap of black and blond. Nutmeg lies on the comforter, her snores harmonizing with Jones who's slumped in a chair beside the bed.

Jones and the lab and I – we're all the same color.

My mind and body are still fuzzy. I'd forgotten about the prednisone puffy feeling, it's been so long since I used my epipens.

This is not the sewing room, not that I'm complaining. The snoozing dog pins my legs in place. I wiggle them free and stretch out across the giant bed.

Mrs. Hawkins arrives carrying a tray filled with coffee, fruit, and muffins. "Good morning!"

Jones wakes up when Mrs. Hawkins shoos Nutmeg to the floor and sets the food down. "Don't you worry. I did the baking myself and everything is allergen free."

I scootch my butt up till I'm sitting, grateful for the support of the headboard.

She fluffs the pillows behind me. "Jones, there's plenty for you, too."

"Good morning." He takes a muffin and a cup of coffee. "Thanks, Davida."

I'm not sure I have an appetite, but with Jones and Mrs. Hawkins watching me, I don't have a choice.

The dogs rush toward the door, tails wagging, woofing a welcome. My mother stands there, fingers worrying a spot on her arm. Beside her is my grandmother, the set of her jaw pulling her mouth into a frown.

My stomach tightens and I force it to relax. "I didn't do anything wrong!" Unless they count eating the pizza.

They sit on the bed, one on each side of me. I swivel my head back and forth, looking from one to the other.

Tucking a braid behind my ear, my mom says, "I'm so sorry. We had no idea you'd gone anaphylactic."

I swat her hand. "You could have checked for messages on your cell phone." Except it was in the sewing room.

Pushing an inquisitive canine away from the food, my grandmother says, "I'm not used to being available all the time. My staff is capable of handling emergencies."

Mrs. Hawkins places the tray on the dresser. "Jones did quite well, I'd say." She walks out of the room with a wink and a smile from the barn manager.

My mom's fretting fingers smooth the wrinkles in the blanket. "Honey, when we came home late last night, you were asleep."

My grandmother awkwardly pats my leg. "I'd like to know what happened."

I tell the story, emphasizing the role of the mean girls, but there is no way to avoid the fact that the fault is mine. "I thought I'd been careful for so long, one little bite wouldn't matter. I didn't know I was allergic to anchovies."

My mom looks at me with a confusing mix of worry and laughter. "You're not."

Jones stands knee-deep in dogs. "It was the shrimp."

Relief races through me. It wasn't my fault. "Who puts shrimp on a pizza?"

My mother leans in close and murmurs, "Welcome to the right coast."

"I'll have a talk with those girls!" My grandmother's voice is stern as a riding whip. "Who gave you the pizza?"

"But they'll just hate me even more. Besides, they didn't know I was allergic." What can I tell her? It was Aqua-girl, Fuchsia, and Violet. Or was it Pansy?

Deep creases appear around her eyebrows and I'm thankful her anger isn't directed at me. "Someone has to pay for this catastrophe!" She squeezes my hand, hard. "Jones, we have some business to discuss."

He takes a quick swig of coffee and kisses me on the forehead. "Come see Dusty when you're up to it," he whispers and follows my grandmother into the hall.

Grandmother takes his hands in hers and speaks softly, but I hear her say, "Thank you, Ezekiel."

Realizing I am in a ruffled nightgown three sizes too big, I ask, "Where are my clothes?"

Grandmother Swift drops Jones's hands, the labs crowding around her legs. "Child, your clothes are in the dresser. From now on, you'll be staying in this room."

"Thank you, Grandmother." It is the first time she smiles at me.

When they leave, my mom and I are alone.

She pours herself a cup of coffee. "Well, it looks like your grandmother's warming up to you."

"At least I'm not sleeping in the sewing room." My voice rises in volume and sarcasm. "It's not like you needed to say anything. You in your periwinkle palace."

She looks across the bed, at the floor, out the window, anywhere, but at me. "Rainbeau, do we have to argue?"

A burst of anger burns so hot it could set the sheets on fire. "Why don't you ever stick up for me?"

My mom stands, smoothing her tight khaki skirt. "Give her time. Your grandmother has to get used to you."

"You didn't answer my question. Besides, what's there to get used to? I'm her granddaughter."

"She's having a hard time."

"What about me? I'm not a bad person." Have I convinced her? Or Grandmother? Or myself?

Her words, "Don't you understand?" are barely whispered. "No!"

"Do we look alike?" Mom asks.

Goosebumps pimple down my arms. "You mean I'm adopted?"

"Of course not. I sweated and screamed you into this world."

I swing my legs over the side of the bed, but I'm still too shaky to stand.

She tucks me back in. "Look at us." My mom's hand is so pale, tiny blue veins pulse beneath the skin.

"My hand is smaller and darker. So?"

"In Eugene, skin color didn't really matter."

She's right. We studied racism in school, but it meant more to the teachers than it did to the kids. News flash: people are different. Big deal.

But last night it was a big deal. The girls were teasing about color. "Mom, it's stupid. If you lined up ten white people all of them would have different skin tones."

She rubs her finger across my tattoo, over and over. "Yes, that's true. But to some people it matters."

"To Grandmother?"

My mom's sigh is so long I wonder when she'll run out of air. "She's trying to find her way. All her friends believe my having a baby with your father was a horrible choice."

My head still feels like it's stuffed with strands of yarn. "Why does she care what her friends think?"

"You care about what Amber thinks. Your grandmother has had the same friends for over fifty years."

I do not belong in a mansion, on a horse farm, in a puny little state filled with people who have big ideas about themselves. "Why did we come here? Grandmother's not even sick."

"It was time."

My muscles tense, the dragon of an argument begins to rise. "I don't fit in here. Maybe it's right for you, but it's wrong for me."

Her silence spurs me on.

"I hate it here. I want to go home." I want to march out the door. I want to make her understand. But I am stuck, stuck, stuck.

"Honey, sometimes a parent has to make a decision that's hard on a child and hope it works out for the best."

"Best for you."

"Best for us. That doesn't mean it's easy."

It isn't easy for me, but maybe it isn't easy for her either. Leaving the yurt, giving up drugs, whatever happened when I was stuck in the pervert and tatted-cat-lady motel.

The fire of arguing has puffed out of me, leaving cool, blue-green tired.

We sit in silence for a while. It's quiet here: bird song, the occasional horse whinny. At home, there were cars and trains and the puppy mill.

"Mom, can we take my braids out?"

She slides off a tiny rubber band and her fingers unwind the tightly woven hair. Each bright colored bead pings as she places it in a dove-shaped china bowl on the nightstand.

I pluck the beads from a braid on the other side of my head. We work together, breathing deeply, relaxing.

When we're done, I look in the mirror. A halo of hair springs up around my head Giggling, I try to pat it down and fail.

My mom stands behind me, her hands on my shoulders.

"Maybe you should shower." She gives me a hug: long and hard and loving. And for once, it doesn't feel like she's taking one.

I stand under the hot pelting drops and wash away angry grime, hospital dirt, and yoga sweat. A wave of release flows from my head to my toes. Tight muscles relax and where the tension used to be the spaces are filled with thankfulness.

"Thank you!"

I'm not sure who I'm thanking. Maybe God.

The stream of wet heat mingles with my tears. "Please help Grandmother love me."

Thankfulness and pleas, maybe those are my prayers.

Nineteen

The next morning, I am still banished to the bedroom. The entire household gangs up and insists that I rest another day. I am convinced forced convalescence is making me crazy.

I sit in the window seat, my sketchpad on my lap and watch the horses in the paddocks. Jones leads Dusty into the nearest one, unclips her lead, and waves to me. I'd love to trade shuffling around in my new blue bathrobe for Dusty's bouncy trot.

Three pages with sketches of Dusty: grazing and galloping, rollicking and rolling. It is so hard to draw horses. No wonder so many tattoo artists do a crappy job.

I can't seem to get the proportions correct. I'll have to study anatomy to get it right. Maybe horses will be my shop's speciality.

Shape, erase. Sketch, erase. Shade.

If horses are in my blood, like Jones said, then why is everything about them difficult?

Knock. Knock. Knock.

"Come in."

Mrs. Hawkins is determined to fatten me up.

Except it isn't the cook.

Or my mom.

"Troy!"

He rushes toward me, his smile brightening the already sunny room.

I jump up, realize I am in my bathrobe and pull it tight. Troy grabs me in a giant hug. His ribs press and poke, his arms are strong against my back. He smells of soap and dogs and safety. The hug is long enough for something to snap inside my chest and I begin to cry.

He reaches for the box of tissues and stumbles over my backpack. "Hey, I thought you'd be happy to see me." Gently, awkwardly, he smoothes my puffy hair.

Why am I crying?

I am an idiot.

Anger and sadness, relief and joy race around inside me like miniature horses on a rampage. "I...I...am glad...really."

He sits on the window seat, long legs stretched almost to the bed. "I can tell."

I stand by the bed. I will not think about the bed.

"You're here. Your dad?" Is my brain working? Apparently not.

"My dad's fine. He went back to work."

"And you're here!" Brain still not functioning.

Ginger strolls in and curls up by Troy's cowboy boots. Obviously old pals.

194

"They didn't want me hitchhiking across the country. So I flew." He scans my sketchbook and gives me a thumbs up. "I heard this place needs a stable hand. Worth quitting smoking to be around horses again."

"Nobody told me you were coming."

His voice is husky, "Surprise."

"So what do you think of the castle of the evil grandmother?"

Troy rubs Ginger's belly. "Evil?"

"Well, maybe not evil, but she hates me, so what's the difference?"

Ginger pumps her back paws, fast enough to catch a squirrel. He rubs her ears instead. "Hates you?"

I hold out my arm.

He tips his head, one eyebrow raised.

"My dad's black, her friends don't like it."

"Racist?" He wraps his hand around his chin and taps his lips with his finger. "I'm surprised. Louise seems really nice."

"You met her?" It's weird having Troy in my room, weird that I am in my bathrobe, weirder that he met my grandmother.

"She set it up."

The weirdest of the weird. She hates me and she sends me him. There is no way I will ever understand my grandmother.

He gazes around the room.

Rumpled bed. Dove dish with beads from my braids. Neat pile of freshly laundered clothes, panties and size double–A bra folded on top.

My cheeks flame, followed by my neck, my chest and other parts of my anatomy that I do not want to think about right now.

"Troy!"

He turns just in time. "What?"

Bra trumps bathrobe.

I steer him toward the door, Ginger between us. "I'll get dressed and give you the tour."

"I thought you had to stay in bed?"

"I'm fine. It's been twenty-four hours." I am such a liar.

The door closes and I race to the offending pile, throwing on each piece before someone comes to stop me.

The rest of the morning is a whirl of introductions: people, horses, dogs. Troy strides through the day, smiling, confident, belonging. By evening he is haying and helping to bring in the horses.

I am ready to rest, but first I make sure Grandmother didn't put Troy in the sewing room. He wouldn't fit on the bed.

A xylophone sounds at six a.m. I turn the alarm off on the phone, dress, and head for the barn. Jones has Dusty ready for me when I arrive.

Troy is not around. This is a good thing. He doesn't need to see me embarrass myself.

We start on the lunge line, but I long to be off leash. "I can do this on my own."

Jones doesn't unhook us. "Warm up first."

We walk, we trot. There is so much to think about: relax your legs – don't squeeze the horse with them, keep your elbows bent, use your hands separately, eyes look straight ahead – not at the ground.

Jones says, "Halt." The pony listens.

He walks towards us, giving me a pep talk. "Remember,

you're the one in control. If she spooks and runs, yank her head around, hard. Don't be afraid to fight."

Fight? This is encouragement?

We walk around and around the ring until I relax. Confident, I touch Dusty with my heels. "Trot."

Bounce, bounce, bounce.

"Feel the rhythm and count the strides."

He counts with me, "One, two, one, two."

Jones jogs along side of us. "Now pick your butt up on "one" and set it back in the saddle on "two.""

I wobble, I grab the saddle, I don't fall off.

"Swing your hips."

Easy peasy. Sort of.

It's still a little bouncy, but when my hips swing in rhythm and my butt goes up and down – I am riding. "I'm doing it!"

"You've got it, girl!"

We circle the ring three times before walking. Dusty and I are a centaur, or maybe a Pegasus – so light we could fly.

Jones says, "Let's head outside. I want to video your ride."

"Why?"

"You can learn a lot watching a video of yourself."

"And hearing you tell me to keep my butt in the saddle. Again."

He holds Dusty's bridle while I dismount. I lead the pony down the aisle, through the doors, to the ring outside. The sun perches in full-blown glory above the horizon.

Jones gives me a leg up, pitching me onto Dusty's back.

I squeeze my legs, urging the pony forward. "Let's go!"
A cool breeze blows, stirring the sand of the arena.

Dusty obliges, trotting around the ring. Her neck curves and she lifts her feet high.

The video! Is the pony showing off for the video?

I focus on rising out of the saddle, up…down…up…down. Every stride challenges my concentration.

"Much better!" Jones shouts. "Flow with the movement of the horse. Don't work so hard."

I try to relax and let it happen, pushing my heels down to counterbalance the upward motion.

From behind the video camera, Jones says, "Close your eyes."

I do it without thinking. Except for the awkward moments when I lose my balance, Dusty and I move together in a dance, supple and smooth.

Lightness fills me and the sun pours into my soul. "Thank you, God."

Eyes open, I turn the corner to head back to Jones. Mom and Grandmother stand beside him crying.

Tension crashes in on me. My muscles tighten and squeeze and my heart races faster than any trot. Dusty responds, picking up the pace into a different, smooth gait.

When we reach them, I pull the pony to a stop. "What's wrong?"

My mom answers, "Nothing!"

"You're riding!" Grandmother is even less helpful.

They both begin to laugh.

Jones adds, "You've never cantered before!"

My family, blue ribbon winners all for stating the obvious.

I smooth the hair on Dusty's neck. "Was I that bad?"

Grandmother steps into the ring, a grin rearranging the wrinkles on her face.

My mom kisses Dusty's nose. "My old friend." She looks up at me. "Rainbeau, it's amazing. You've never ridden before!"

My legs tighten and the pony tosses her head. "Jones has been teaching me."

A look of amusement passes between my teacher and my grandmother. She says, "Dear, most people can't canter that well after only two lessons."

A compliment from Grandmother! Her reaction isn't anything like what I'd expected. I swing my right leg over Dusty's back, dismounting before I fall off and ruin everything.

My mom is on one side and Grandmother is on the other. We walk to the barn talking about horses and I imagine the three of us riding through the woods together.

Riding horses is my new happy dance.

Jones stops by the tack room to talk with Grandmother. I lead Dusty down the aisle to her stall.

Rounding a corner, I halt, Dusty beside me.

Aqua-girl, long and lean in her breeches and polo shirt, is too close to Troy for my comfort. They stand by a gray mare who is blocking the aisle.

"Do you think you could help me?" she asks in a voice of sugarcoated arsenic.

Troy smiles, seemingly oblivious to her black widow charms. "Sure. Sometimes they puff up and it's tough to tighten the girth."

She lays her hand on his arm and tips her head toward his. "You are so sweet."

The only trick she's missing is batting eyelashes.

I'd like to bat her. If envy is green, then I must be pure, shining emerald.

Troy unclips the cross-ties. "Do you want me to hold her while you mount? I can check it once you're on."

I am grubby from riding: sweat stains and helmet hair. Even at my best I can't compete with miss-long-legs-blond-hair-beautiful. My heart shrinks and I wish my whole body would shrink as well so I could scamper away without being noticed.

But then Troy turns and grins at me. "Hey, Beau!"

"Oh," says Aqua-girl, "Do you know Shrimp?" Her laughter is tinkly fake and she leads the mare forward, blocking my view of Troy, taking him with her.

I spend a long time grooming Dusty, careful not to brush my emotions across her body. The phrase, "angry enough to spit nails" comes to mind and I realize why – I taste iron, blood iron. The cuticle on my middle finger no longer exists. I have ingested skin and horse hair and dirt and I do not care.

I know Troy is two years older than me. I know Aqua-girl is probably his age and she is beautiful and she is a bitch. I do not know if Troy likes her.

Or me.

Why would he choose me over her?

Maybe boys don't mind girls who are bitchy.

I dig the dirt out of Dusty's hooves with a vengeance. When I sweep the aisle such a cloud of dust rises, even the pony sneezes. I put her in her stall and feed her an apple, but my mind is still on Aqua-girl.

I change into shorts, leaving my breeches and boots in

the viewing room closet. Troy must still be with her because I haven't seen him.

As I leave the barn an entire conversation runs through my mind, telling Troy exactly what I think about Aqua-girl.

I could innocently begin, "You know it was me she tried to kill?"

Twenty

I head for the woods, stomping through the tall grass: swish, swish, swish. Sneakers protect my feet, but my bare legs are scratched at each step. Maybe I shouldn't have taken off the breeches and boots.

If only I had Troy's attention, Troy's affection, and a punching bag.

Thoughts roil through my head and I am almost in the woods before I'm aware of people talking.

I can't hear words. I can hear anger.

Crouching down and searching, I see bright colors beyond the first few trees.

A woman screams, "No, Robert!"

It's my mom.

My legs carry me forward before my brain registers that I am running. Too far to see them clearly, but close enough to hear another voice I recognize. "You do have my money, bitch."

Oyster. How could I have forgotten he was coming here?

Crumbling before they notice me, I curl into a ball on the ground. Echoes of Oyster: tongue in my ear, hand on my breast, body hard pressed against my belly. I sink into myself.

My mother begs, "I don't know what you're talking about."

"The urn." His voice growls, sand grating my soft insides, "My money is gone."

She is silent.

I hear a hiss, my name on the tongue of a snake, "Rainbeau, the thief."

"Don't hurt her. Please. I'll get you the money and more."

More? What more? More money? Or?

Slap! Loud as a shot. Birds take flight, winging over the woods.

My mother sobs.

Oyster's voice lowers, "I'll kill her."

Meaning me.

No!

Power fills me. Hardening blood and bone, sinew and self. I will not give in. I grab a dead branch and rush toward them.

This time is different. This time I won't be a victim. This time I am strong and I will fight.

Lungs and heart pump strength through my veins. Now, now, now!

Three more steps toward him and I swing my weapon at his head. He turns and it smashes into his face, nose blooming brilliant burgundy. Grunting, he tears it out of my hands. Splinters rake my palms.

He swipes the branch at me and I duck. It catches in the crux of a tree and cracks in half, shards of wood and bark explode. He yanks, trying to wrench it free.

Anger courses through me, blood on fire. Attack! I rage toward him, teeth bared, nails ripping the flesh on his cheek.

Beating, pounding. "You will not hurt my mother."

He smacks me. We are so close his stink is in my nostrils.

I slam harder. Soft, private parts. "I hate you!"

Lunging toward me, grabbing, holding. His fingers bruise my biceps. He wraps his arms around me, a viper's vice squeezing my ribs. "The mouse that roared."

I am anger. I am fight. I am rage.

Kicking ankles and thighs. One arm free, I scramble for his eyes. His grip loosens.

I struggle and get away, searching for a weapon. "You will not hurt me!"

Grabbing a club-sized branch from the underbrush, I hammer his head, smash his sternum.

My mother's whimpers barely register.

Oyster begs, "Stop, please." Red blends into his button-down shirt, stains his jeans, coats the stubble on his chin – blood red.

I don't stop. "I'll kill you!"

The world stills, except for the strikes.

The weapon grows heavy in my hands. A guttural animal grunt sounds in rhythm with the blows and I realize I am the animal.

Enough.

Vision clear of the blood lust, but the desire to hurt him still pumps through my veins. "You will not touch me or my mother. Ever!"

He doesn't answer.

He doesn't look at me.

He doesn't move.

A rivulet of red runs down his head, past his ear, pools on a leaf.

I hold fast to the feeling of power, of rage. I want to smear that greasy black hair with more blood.

My mother takes my hand, babbling, "I'm so sorry, so sorry." She sobs as she pulls me away through the woods.

Exhaustion overtakes me. I follow without thinking, limbs leaden, mind numb.

The road. Stone beneath my sneakers. A cloud of dust approaches. The hunter-green farm truck moves toward us down the driveway and slides to a stop. Troy, Grandmother, and Jones leap out – shouting.

I drop the club and Troy wraps his arms around me. Shaking, my entire body is caught in a vortex of emotion that I cannot control. Worse than when I fell in the Mississippi, worse than when I had to drive, worse than the shrimp pizza.

His fingers are touching my face. It stings and I whip my head back. "Beau, you're bleeding."

Jones wraps my mother in a horse blanket. She is mumbling. Grandmother kneels before me. "Darling, what happened?"

"Oyster attacked."

She looks away, toward my mother. "They're both incoherent."

Troy sits on the ground pulling me into my lap. "No, Oyster is Star's boyfriend."

Jones says, "Come again?"

I rest my head on Troy's shoulder. He explains, "Elizabeth's boyfriend – Robert."

Grandmother gently sweeps the hair out of my eyes. "Rainbeau, where is he?"

I nod toward the woods. It's the best I can do.

She throws Troy her cell. "Call 911." She opens the back door of the pick-up and grabs a shotgun. "Let's go, Ezekiel."

My body, so hard before, is boneless, soft as tofu. Troy calls the police, asks for an ambulance, checks on my mother. I shiver underneath a brown and blue checkered horse blanket.

Lights flash. Sirens screech. Police cars. Ambulances. Fire trucks. Who knew there were so many emergency vehicles in Westwood?

These paramedics are kind, gentle fingers making sure I am not broken. They wash the blood off my skin, amazed that most of it isn't mine. Only a cut by my eye. No stitches needed.

I huddle under my horse blanket sanctuary, surrounded by the dusty animal smell. Troy squats by my side, so close the toe of his dirty cowboy boot presses against my thigh.

From the woods, we hear crackling leaves and breaking branches. An officer and a paramedic carry Oyster on a stretcher. Jones and Grandmother follow, the shotgun by her side.

Oyster's eyes are closed and his mouth hangs open, so bloody I must have knocked out some of his teeth.

I spit a glob of phlegm in his direction. "No tooth fairy for him."

Troy hugs me, his cheek resting on my head. "God and his fairies were watching over you."

God and fairies? There's a new idea.

They load Oyster into an ambulance and a policeman climbs in with him. A squad car follows them down the driveway.

I lean into Troy.

A male and a female officer argue with Grandmother about questioning me at the station. Their good cop/bad cop routine doesn't work. Grandmother wins and we drive to the house.

The EMTs assure me that my mother was not injured. They carry her up the stairs, Mrs. Hawkins trailing behind. They will give my mom something to help her sleep.

Will she relapse?

Life with her on drugs. Again.

"God, please don't let her choose the drugs instead of me this time," I murmur.

We sit in the den on the leather couches. Easier to clean off the blood. Troy is next to me, his arm around me. I wish … nevermind.

I am in trouble. The police officers are here and they will take me away. My heart plods: theft, assault, theft, assault. The adults discuss matters, but I don't bother to listen. I know I am guilty.

I think about stealing Oyster's money after he molested me. And about giving the money to Troy so he could see his dad in the hospital. Would I make different choices, if I could? No.

I think about attacking Oyster in the woods after he hit my mom. Of maybe killing him. Anything different? No.

Grandmother sits beside me, holding my hand in her strong, rough palm. "This nice officer has a few questions."

She might be nice now, but she won't be when she finds out what I've done. Briefly, I consider lying. Troy and Grandmother watch me.

I can't lie any longer.

I lift my hand to bite my cuticles, but my fingers are covered in blood. His blood. "Did I kill him?"

Murder is a different pile of horse poop.

Grandmother squeezes my hand till the bones pop and I am sure the answer is, yes. Then I remember her heading to the woods with a gun. Maybe she killed him. Should I take the blame? I would, but she had the gun and I was covered in blood.

Thoughts weigh me down and all I want to do is sleep.

The officer says, "Rainbeau, he's beat pretty bad, but he's alive. And he'll stay that way until his trial." The hard edge in her voice leaves me wondering if she'd prefer him dead. She must be familiar with creeps like him.

Then, in a voice suddenly soothing, practiced at extracting information, she says, "Tell me what happened."

My insides knot, worse than a horse with colic. Will Troy hate me for stealing? Will Grandmother? The story takes a long time to tell, even though I don't mention what Oyster did to me. I can't. Troy, my mom, Grandmother – how could they love someone who's been molested?

They listen without a sound.

The tale ends with me describing the slap and beating Oyster into a stew of mud. I don't describe how I felt.

My audience is wriggling: legs cross and uncross, seats shift and glances pass. The barest whisper on my lips, "What kind of person am I that I beat someone bruised and bloody?"

My grandmother leans close. "Honest and brave."

"Where was God?"

"By your side helping you protect yourself and your mother."

Mr. Hawkins sets sandwiches and tea on the table. "And though she but little, she is fierce." He hands my grandmother a teacup. "*A Midsummer Night's Dream*. Shakespeare."

I have to ask, "Do they put handcuffs on teenagers?"

The officer pats my thigh like it's a puppy. "You're not going to jail."

The policeman at the door looks like he'd be more comfortable holding a football than a cup of tea. "Definitely self-defense."

"What about the money in the urn?"

The policewoman leans back in her chair and breathes the thin tendrils of steam from the teacup Hawkins hands her. "It's up to Oyster...Robert to press charges."

Grandmother slams her cup onto the saucer. "I'll take care of that."

I curl closer to Troy, confident she will.

Twenty-one

In the morning, I find Grandmother's hot tub on its own patio. I take a deep rose-scented breath. Pale pink blooms climb the trellises attached to the privacy screens.

I slide into the steaming, bubbling water. It melts away the aches, soreness, and images of yesterday.

Last night before bed, Mrs. Hawkins came to say goodnight. "Think about five good things about the day when you get up in the morning and five more when you go to bed at night."

Number one – I'll ride Dusty this afternoon. Two – Troy offered to take me into town for a sorbet after my lesson. The hot tub is definitely number three.

Washing away the chaos and confusion, I sink beneath the surface. Weightless and warm, I float free. My mind lingers over the last two weeks – a crazy palette of fear and faith and family.

There is still one color not quite right.

Good things number four and five will have to wait. I turn off the jets, step out of the tub, and wrap myself in a giant striped towel.

Up the stairs to my room, careful not to drip on the floor. The air is so filled with moisture, completely dry doesn't happen even with a humongous towel. I change into cut-offs and a tie-dye t-shirt, my feet bare.

Digging through my pack, I find the tiny statue of Dusty.

I drag my feet on the slick wood floors, forcing myself down the stairs. Maybe Grandmother is gone for the day.

She isn't.

I stand by the door of her office while she types, waiting. Waiting until she finishes. Until she notices me.

But she doesn't turn around.

I am charcoal gray fear. Waiting.

An idea pops into my brain turning me inspired sunshine yellow.

I race back upstairs. Thoughts and images of an apology on paper. So much better than a simple, "I'm sorry."

In my room, my sketchbook and pencils are laid out on the window seat. I wonder about Grandmother's favorite colors. Mostly, she wears black breeches and a white riding shirt. But, the bowl in the kitchen is cobalt, the office walls are indigo, the pillows in the den, midnight.

I choose my favorite pencils, shorter than the rest. Next, I need to decide whether I apologize for taking the figure or thank her for taking care of me. Doodling, letting words float onto the page, a poem takes shape.

I have always wanted
A real family
Searching across the country
For what was not to be
You were cold and distant
No cookies did you bake
Riding is your passion
A granddaughter to forsake
Horses, dogs, and Oyster
Always so very near
I learned to be strong
To conquer my fear
Through crisis after crisis
Shrimp pizza and shellfish
You came through when I needed you
To fulfill my wish.

First, I sketch a Celtic border, adding elaboration as I move along the page. When it is finished, I lightly trace the poem in the center. It takes a few tries to line it up just right. I create my own font as I work in the colors, curling ends of letters, thickening stems and curves. Hours pass and my drawing is detailed, vivid, finished.

Back down the front stairs, my hand dances around the banister's spirals.

Grandmother is reading something on her computer, no longer typing. When she turns and smiles at me, I see sparkle and sprite.

She ushers me into her office, swiveling in her chair. But I don't sit on the deep-cushioned recliner. There is one question I must ask before apologizing. I need to know the answer before I find out if she is angry at me for being a thief.

That scrunchy feeling in my chest has returned. My breath comes in short trotting-Dusty gasps. "Grandmother, do you hate me because I'm half-black?"

The word dynamites from her mouth, "No!"

She pulls me to her, holding my moist hands in her strong, dry ones. "Child, I couldn't dislike you because of the color of your skin."

"But Mom said, your friends …"

"Yes, well, unfortunately, I do have some friends who are not so open-minded, but I don't give a rat's ass what they think."

"Really?" Happiness is a gallop through a green pasture. Grandmother loves me more than the friends she's had for fifty years!

She nods, a smile easing the tension in her face.

"I'm so sorry, Grandmother."

I hand her the poem, holding my breath, hoping she'll like it.

"You've got a lot of talent. Why waste it on tattoos?"

An argument sits on my tongue waiting for me to open my mouth. Instead, I swallow and open my hand.

She plucks the pony off my palm. "Do you know why this is important to me?"

My eyes flicker to the collection above her computer. "No. You have so many I thought you wouldn't notice."

"Rainbeau, each of these is special because they were given to me by the man I love."

"Grandfather?"

"No. Our parents insisted we marry, but we wouldn't have chosen each other. Over time we grew to appreciate, to love one another in our own way." She points to the tiny equines lining her office. "One each year, on my birthday."

There must be forty figurines. And then I know who has been with Grandmother that long. Not Grandfather. Not Mom. Not me. "Jones."

"Ezekiel. Yes."

"Does he know you love him?"

"No, dear." Her sigh is resignation, rather than anguish. "He's worked for me all these years. How could I tell him?"

This time I close my hands around hers. "We'll find a way!"

"No need for you to worry about that!" The sun shines through the window, glinting off her hair like a helmet. She picks up a pair of riding gloves from the desk. "Time to ride!"

My Grandmother Swift: straight, strong, and tough.

I follow her to the front door. She stops with her hand on the knob, staring at my feet.

They are clean.

"Shoes." She points to a pair of pistachio colored loafers with gems, glued to the front, tasteful of course. "A must at the barn."

Do I wear them without socks?

The tensing of her muscles tells me grandmother is impatient to get to the barn. I slip on the shoes, soft comfortable leather wraps around my feet.

Is this what shoes are supposed to feel like?

I walk double-quick to keep up with Grandmother's stride.

She reminds me of a wild mustang sensing freedom.

The silence between us is comfortable – no unnecessary questions filling up space. That doesn't mean I don't have any, just for now it feels better not to ask.

When we reach the barn, Jones is standing in the aisle holding a huge black horse. Grandmother's touch is tender as she takes the reins from his hand.

I want to shout, "She loves you!" But I don't.

The horse steps forward, his gigantic feet headed my way. I press up against a stall door. "Loafers aren't much protection against those."

Grandmother pats the animal's shoulder. "Probably not, but horses carry tetanus and shoes will protect any cuts on your feet. You have had your shots, haven't you?"

I shrug, knowing by the end of the day Grandmother will have taken care of that and any other diseases I could possibly be carrying.

The clop-clop of hooves resounds on the cement as they head down the aisle to the outdoor ring. When will Grandmother tell Jones her true feelings?

I give them some space, just in case, and duck into the tack room.

Troy.

"Hey, Beau!" He throws a sponge at me.

I take the hint and start cleaning tack. My heart beats happy. We settle into a rhythm, talk about horses.

Finished, he hangs a bridle on a hook. "Come see your grandmother ride."

We walk outside to the ring. At the rail, I close my eyes

remembering his arms wrapped around me. No, this is different. I open my eyes and slide away.

He moves closer, elbow touching my ribs.

Can he tell I'm melting? I focus on the sand and the sky and the horse.

Pirate music begins. Loud pirate music. Very loud pirate music.

Grandmother trots around the ring, regal and serene. No bouncing black pony. They halt and there is silence. A moment later, the music begins again and with it a dance. The beats are perfectly timed to the horse's hooves touching the ground.

Grandmother and the black trot in place. The horse's legs are suspended, defying gravity. Then they glide sideways across the ring. At a big letter 'C' they canter. Thundering past us, ending in an impossibly small pirouette. Down the far side, the Black lifts his legs so high they seem to float across the diagonal of the ring. Impossible.

Troy reaches over and squeezes my fingers. "Dressage."

The routine lasts the length of a long song, but each moment is glorious. The transformation of two beings into one: divine.

The music ends, but they continue to work on some of the moves. Can you perfect perfection?

My mom walks over and gives my shoulder a squeeze. "They're something to watch, aren't they?"

"Amazing!"

She glances at Troy, then me and smiles.

I shiver, icy in the sunshine. She knows I like Troy? When did that happen?

Grandmother drops her reins and they walk over to us. The Black is covered in flecks of foamy sweat.

"Grandmother, you were amazing!"

She pats her horse's neck. "Freestyle dressage. My passion."

I reach my hand toward the giant Black. "What's your horse's name?"

"*Cambiare*. It means 'change.'"

Troy whispers, his breath tickling my ear, "Not always a bad thing."

I lean into him, just a little. "Will I ever be able to ride like that?"

Grandmother gathers up the reins. "It takes a lot of hard work. Let's see how you do at your first show."

"Show?"

"In August."

Maybe she won't send me away.

Troy wraps his arm around my shoulders. He grins that goofy, exasperating, endearing smile. "The girl who didn't even like dogs!"

Six weeks to go from bounce-bounce-bouncing to riding in a horse show?

Why not?

I've improvised, adapted, and overcome: driven a car, squashed an Oyster, and found my family.

I'm good to go and good to stay.

About the Author

Gail Fischer

Cerredwyn grew up in the horse and art worlds. In college, she studied psychology, English, biology, anthropology, and theatre, and almost didn't get her degree when she angered the administration. She managed to graduate and continued her studies in Eastern religions, advanced mathematics, textiles, and psychopharmacology. The eclectic course selection confused her professors and she did not complete her master's.

While living in Vienna, she wrote a document on cocaine for the United Nations and waltzed at a masked ball at the Hofburg Palace. In Oregon, she worked as a journalist for local and national magazines. Her favorite assignment was interviewing New Age gurus. She also enjoyed her time as a mounted security officer and coloring flash in a tattoo shop.

Her current life consists of spending time with her beloved husband and awesome daughter. She can be found leading a Girl Scout troop, substitute teaching, and occasionally bellydancing. She also trains her dressage horse, sings in a choir, and reads avidly. As an entrepreneur, she edits numerous books, meets with designers, chooses marketing plans, signs contracts, does school visits and book signings, and of course, writes.

Only in hindsight have the disparate elements of her life begun to make sense.

 Contact the Author

cr@cerredwyn.com

Book Two Coming Soon:

Rainbeau Harley Swift

10% of the profits from the sale of the Rainbeau Harley books
will be donated to 501(c)(3) non-profit organizations.

Who do you think Rainbeau would choose to donate to?
Help decide where the money will go.

cerredwyn.com

Would you like to contribute
to the enhanced E-book of Rainbeau Harley?

Music to go with her songs?
Rainbeau inspired poetry?
A video you've directed?

cr@cerredwyn.com

Made in the USA
Lexington, KY
16 July 2013